THIS JEALOUS EARTH

STORIES

MG Press
http://midwestgothic.com/mgpress

Portions of this book originally appeared in *Anomalous, The Carleton
Voice, Best Indie Lit New England, Chamber Four, Ducts, Eunoia
Review, Every Writer Resource Short Stories*, Lit-Cast.com, *The
MacGuffin, Midwestern Gothic, Prime Number, Red Ochre Press,
Short Fiction Collective* and *Spilling Ink*.

ISBN: 978-1480172777

Cover design © 2012 Sarah E Melville, Sleeping Basilisk Graphic Design

Author photo © Paul Carpenter

THIS JEALOUS EARTH

STORIES

SCOTT DOMINIC CARPENTER

MG PRESS

For what other life was he saving up before expressing, at long last, his true feelings about things, before crafting opinions he didn't need to put in quotes, before ceasing to devote himself, with punctilious decorum, to endeavors that he claimed at the same time to be ridiculous?

— Marcel Proust, *Swann's Way*

THE
TENDER
KNIFE

THE NIGHT BEFORE THE KILLING, Walter plucked silverware out of the dishwasher and thunked it into the drawer. Next to the slotted tray, other utensils caught his eye—the steak knives, the paring knife, the chef's knife, the cleaver.

"It's like the guillotine," Dale had told him, drawing a finger across his own throat. "Fast. Efficient. Painless. If you love 'em, that's what you'll do."

Walter looked down at his hands, liver-spotted and trembling. He made a fist and held it tight. Perhaps he could be equal to this task. He'd put it off so many times. Whenever Julia talked about it, he'd feel a twinge of foreboding. Or perhaps it was a throb of angina. And then he'd bend the conversation to something else.

Tonight he had set the steaks to marinate long before she returned home from showing houses. It was the week before Christmas, but unseasonably hot, and they had dinner on the flagstone patio next to the barbecue, in the shade of the ash tree, close to the desert willow and the blooming yarrow. As they drained a bottle of Sauvignon Blanc, Julia had melted from a senior realtor back into a woman—a dark-haired, still-slender, still-lovely woman.

There'd been that lilt to her voice that hinted at desire. They'd lingered over dinner, Walter refilling her glass from the sweating bottle, the air freshening as the sun sank toward the crest of the San Gabriel Mountains.

She'd given him that sly look, lowering her lids while her lips tightened.

That's when the tail of a koi had splashed in the pond—the one Walter had dug so many years ago, lining the pit with butyl rubber, pouring the cement base and mortaring the walls. It was the centerpiece of the yard, with a stone path leading to it through the bent grass. The fish were hungry now, growing restless, calling to him.

Julia had glanced at the water, tossing her hair back and wrinkling her nose in that pretty way. Then she'd said it: "You really need to take care of it, honey."

He'd nodded, but only because he hadn't wanted to spoil the mood. Yes, he heard himself say, yes, he would.

And here he was now, studying cutlery in the dishwasher.

What did Dale know? What made their neighbor such an expert?

Take care of it. Such gentle-sounding words. But he knew what they meant. There were too many of the fish. Way too many. And they had grown so much over the years. The pond was nearly twelve feet long—and as deep as his grandson was tall—but it was too cramped, overrun.

As a reward for his promise they made love that night, a heaving, churning ordeal that left him both breathless and grateful, but tinged with the remorse of a bad transaction. Soon Julia drifted off, each of her whistling breaths stealing away a little more of his own slumber. He rose up on his elbow and studied his wife, her neck still soft and smooth, only faint lines by her eyes. What business did he have with this woman, almost fifteen years his junior? Maybe he should never have remarried.

Sleep was hard to come by these days for Walter, a scarce commodity, and what little he found barely deserved the name. It was like wakefulness covered by a threadbare sheet. The wine, which made him drowsy at first, left him restive. Not to mention the sex. So he rolled out of bed, went downstairs and finished cleaning up the kitchen.

When he carried dinner scraps out to the moonlit pond, the koi saw him coming. They thrashed in the water, their different-colored bodies roiling together like the tentacles of a sea monster.

Julia's approach never made them frisky. They knew the difference.

The fish frenzied as he sprinkled chunks of food into the froth, but even then they showed deference, making room for old Gandalf, the white giant, over three feet in length, his tattered tail sweeping like the train of a majestic robe through the water. Walter lowered himself to his knees, holding out a knob of meat at the surface, and as Gandalf took it in his fleshy mouth, the two of them, man and animal, exchanged a glance.

Back inside, Walter pulled the slider closed against the night and was ambushed by his own reflection in the glass. A beefy and slack man in rumpled pajamas. Droopy eyes. Even his mustache gone snowy. He stretched his chin forward to give definition to his jaw. Yes, it was still the same man under there.

He watched a late-night show, read two magazines, started a third, his eyes skating over the pages, the words leaving only a faint residue in his mind. Vague and distant, that was the news—unrelated to life in their neighborhood, its rhythms set by mail deliveries and garbage day, trips to the grocery store and the dry cleaner. There was also the weekly phone call with his son Peter in Chicago, when he could hear the chirps of Sammy and Chloe, those rambunctious grandkids who never seemed to know what to say to him, and he didn't know back, leaving them all to babble silly things back and forth until everyone laughed. What wouldn't he give to see them again, to squeeze their little bodies in his arms. But they were separated by mountains and desert and more mountains, followed by plains. No, he wouldn't do that drive again. And the doctor recommended against flying. Better for them to come to L.A. at Christmas. They'd put up a tree, a real one, pretend that it was winter, pull the stale ornaments out of the basement, with the kids running in the yard, feeding the fish, maybe jumping in Dale's swimming pool next door, squealing, crying out to their grandpa, calling his name with their thin voices: Walter, Walter.

"*Walter*," the voice bleated again, louder.

He startled awake, squinting in the light. Julia towered over him, dressed for work. A sofa cushion jabbed into his back.

She shook her head, glanced at her watch. She had a showing at nine. "Did you spend the whole night down here?"

Probably? His mind was still thick. "No problem," he said.

"Don't worry about me." He attempted to sit up, but his back ached from the sofa. He'd try again in a minute, maybe after she left.

Julia gave him a pinched look. "Are you all right?"

He nodded.

While she fetched her purse, she talked at him. Details about shopping and laundry. Then a moment of grace: she bent down and kissed the top of his head.

On her way out she stopped, turned back, her hand on the doorframe. "Don't forget what we talked about." She nodded toward the patio. "Do take care of it, won't you?"

Take care. Right.

Then she was gone. He heard the car back down the driveway, and with a groan he struggled to his feet, climbed the stairs, changed. After breakfast he swept the kitchen and watered the plants. Halfway through the morning he found himself staring at the letter opener in his hand, dropping it like a murder weapon.

He walked out to the patio and surveyed the blooming garden. Nearly Christmas, but the plants quivered with life. Nothing ever withered here.

As he approached the water, the black speckled fish, the one Sammy had named Pony, saw him first, and soon many of the koi had swarmed to the side: Orange Juice, Tiger, Measles, Cyclops, Frog. On and on. There were twenty-six of them, including Gandalf, the granddaddy of them all, aloof at the side.

Twenty-six. Too many, far too many for this pond. He'd dug it out over two decades ago, and Gandalf was the only survivor from the original batch, his color vanishing when the temperature spiked too high, which left all his companions belly up. That had been the first of three koi holocausts before Walter got the chemicals right and improved the filtration system. Then he'd gotten it under control. Many of the fish had swum in this pool for a decade or more. The population was constant—thank goodness they gobbled up their own young—but individually they kept growing and growing. A couple dozen had seemed about right, even a little skimpy, back when they were small fry. But these koi stretched longer every year, doubling in size, then tripling and quadrupling. Most were now over two feet, a couple closing in on three. And Gandalf the White, that hoary old thing, his fins and tail frayed, was longer than Walter's outstretched arm. Walter had waited for nature to take its course, for mortality to thin the herd. But Death wasn't interested in the koi, leaving them to swim in ever-tighter circles inside their shrinking home.

Then he'd done a little research and discovered why: these fish, they could live for decades, over a hundred years. And they would only grow larger.

He'd never told Julia about the ad he'd placed in the classifieds over a month ago, the one where he'd offered the koi up for adoption. No one had called, and in fact there were two other ads just like his own.

He'd considered letting them loose in the stream in the park. But Dale, who fished and hunted, explained how they'd perish from the shock or die slowly from parasites. It would be a cruel finish. Then he'd outlined the best way, the most responsible and humane: knock them unconscious and cut off their heads, right behind the gills. If Walter really cared about them, he'd help them go fast. He owed them that, didn't he?

Walter had managed to keep his lip from trembling while Dale was there. Then he'd tried to forget about it. But Julia kept prodding. And now he had promised.

He found the net out in the garage, tucked by the old refrigerator where they kept the beer, next to the workbench piled high with tools and jars and rolls of tape. At the side of the pool, the fish vied with one another for the opportunity to draw close, and they glided into the net as though eager to sacrifice themselves for their fellows. Or for Walter himself—traitorous Walter, whom they expected to nourish them. The hard part was choosing who would go and who would stay. Once again the pain rose in his chest. He had no authority to make such decisions, no idea what criteria to use. He could take the oldest first, but since every fish in the pond was built to outlive him, that detail didn't seem relevant. Size, perhaps? He could save more by removing the largest ones—maybe just four or five. But all that would do is buy a little time, stay some executions, and in two or three years he'd have to thin it again. How about color? The two gray ones were invisible against the dark bottom, and Orange Juice disappeared against the tan rock of the sides. Wasn't the whole point to have fish you could see? It was the mottled or striped ones—fish like Tiger and Measles—that stood out the best.

Decisions, he thought. This word brought another: *precision*. Not to mention *incision*. Words of sharpness.

And Julia had left this task to him. *What does it matter?* she'd asked, way back when she first started to nag. *They're just fish.*

What does it matter.

In the end he applied a compromise of all the principles. By turns, old ones and big ones and unmottled ones swam into the mesh, the aluminum handle of the net bowing with the weight as he lifted each one out and dumped it into a plastic tub, joining it with the others. Even then they didn't thrash, just flicked their tails once or twice and settled in, gaping slowly, as though sucking in the warm air. They didn't panic. It was just Walter, after all.

Old Gandalf, nearly translucent, hovered in the middle of the pool, watching the roundup. According to every measure, he too should go. If he didn't, Julia would have something to say about it.

The net nearly buckled when he hoisted that behemoth out of the water. The fish watched as Walter lowered him into the tub and disentangled his fins from the mesh. The whiskery barbels at the sides of his mouth gave him a dour expression.

Walter rested his eyes. A fish, he told himself. Just a fish.

He started with Pony because she was smaller than the others. He wanted something manageable, a trial run. At the patio table, he'd lifted the taut, wriggling body out of the tub, gripping her tail as best he could. *Stun them*, that's what Dale had said. *Then they won't feel a thing.* Gritting his teeth, Walter took a deep breath, aimed and whacked Pony's head against the flagstone, as hard as he dared. And it seemed to work: the fish stopped flopping. Walter lay Pony out on the cutting board brought from the kitchen, and he released his breath. It hadn't been as difficult as he'd feared. Perhaps the blow to the head had already killed her. The rest would just be a formality, an insurance policy.

The knife he'd chosen was a long, slender blade with a black handle, perfect for cutting through onions and potatoes, a compromise between flex and rigidity. After holding the blade over the fish's neck for several seconds, just behind the gills, steeling himself to be hard, to be sharp and fast, he plunged down with a sawing motion. Too late he realized the knife was the wrong choice. The scales were too strong, or his arm too weak. The blade wouldn't cut, and then Pony woke up, a Lazarus fish risen from the dead, thrashing with such force that Walter feared he'd lose his grip. He sawed all the harder, but there was no serration to the edge, nothing to catch on the lip of the scales, and the more he pushed, the more the blade pressed into the flesh, strangling the fish more than beheading it. Walter could barely keep his eyes open, so he stopped, let go, pulled the knife away from Pony's spotted throat only to find that the flesh didn't spring back, that the blade had finally crushed through the scales, opening up a gash through which blood and some other liquid now oozed. Pony writhed and flailed, struggling to live, although even Walter could see that life draining away onto the cutting board.

More mysterious were the strange crescent marks on Pony's underside, where the blade hadn't even touched. Then he understood: he'd clamped her down so hard that his fingernails had driven into her belly. There was no going back now, not after crushing her insides. He clenched his teeth, slapping his left hand back onto the clammy skin of the fish and pinning it down, going at it with the knife, digging away, trying again to push through and finish the job. But the knife stopped against something tough, and the more Walter pushed, the harder Pony thrashed.

He let go again, gasping for breath as he raced back into the house, smearing fish blood on the handle of the slider, yanking open the drawer in the kitchen, retrieving the cleaver. A moment later he was back outside, and then—oh miracle!—Pony was *gone*, vanished, and for an instant Walter's heart lightened. He'd been delivered, spared this sacrifice, as when the angel had stopped Abraham's hand over Isaac.

But no, there she was on the flagstone under the table, where she'd landed after flipping herself off. Pony's head leaned a bit to one side, one eye looking up. Down on his knees, Walter grabbed her again. Holding the fish, he took up the cleaver, hacking almost blindly, his vision blurred. The blade didn't come down flat, and he sent off chips of flagstone. Or chips of Pony. On the third blow, the body went utterly rigid in Walter's hand, then shivered and re-laxed. On the fourth, the head separated from the rest, and Walter, exhausted, dropped the cleaver and fell back onto his rump. His khaki pants were smeared with red ooze. The head was detached but Pony's mouth opened twice more, slowly.

Walter heard himself gasp, then realized he was sobbing. He wiped his face with his sleeve, then looked back at the plastic tub where seven other koi waited, yawning for air. There was no way he could do that again. No way.

"Good grief," Julia said when he called her to report the di-saster. He could tell she was stepping out of earshot of her clients. "They're just fish, Walter," she said, her voice half bewildered, half scolding. "Just take care of it."

There it was again, that expression. The catch-all.

There were voices in the background. "I'm sorry, but I have to go," she said. "I have people waiting."

The phone clicked.

Julia would have lined the koi up like stalks of celery and cut through them all with a single swipe. But she hadn't been the one to feed them, to care for them—not the way he had over the past twenty years.

It was the grandkids who would notice. Chloe would ask what had become of Pony or Orange Juice or Gandalf. What was he to tell her? That he'd decapitated them at the patio table?

He took a break to regroup, washing up in the bathroom, scrub-bing the crusted fluids from his arms and face with a washcloth. He rinsed the spatters of fish blood from his mustache, rubbing the white whiskers, smoothing them down past the corners of his mouth. The man in the mirror looked to him like the butcher of Treblinka.

He made himself a sandwich—avoiding the cutlery drawer—and pondered his next move. The trick was to end it all quickly or painlessly. Both, if possible. No more knives. Dale had guns next door, but Walter couldn't see himself firing a .22 into the heads of fish. After lunch, he checked on the plastic tub, hoping they might have expired on their own, but no, they lay together like giant sardines alive in a can, calmly gasping. How many hours could this go on?

He checked the internet. Yes, just like everything else, there were pages about how to kill koi. He wasn't the first one to face this problem. Opinions varied. Most of them came down on the side of Dale's solution: stun and cut. But a few recommended freezing, which numbed them like an anesthetic. Walter remembered a story he'd read, decades ago, in high school—a man lost in the Yukon. Supposedly it wasn't such a bad way to go. And since fish were cold-blooded to begin with, it made sense. Didn't it?

Out in the garage stood the old fridge, the bottom filled with beer.

He divided the koi into two garbage bags, doubled for strength, the plastic so thick he could barely tie them. Then he hauled them to the garage, each sack heavier than a load of salt. The fridge was an upright model, the freezer on top capacious and nearly empty. As he heaved in the bags, the fish wriggled and slid about, and Walter tucked in the corners of plastic before slamming the door, the magnetic strip sealing them in like the last block of a pharaoh's tomb.

He panted, his face wet. The bags had been heavy but it wasn't that. Something moved in the freezer and an ice cube tray clunked against the inside. Walter stared at the cement floor between his feet. Then he trudged back through the house. On the patio he hosed out the plastic tub and returned it to the garden shed. He wrapped Pony's body parts in another bag, which he sealed with a twist-tie and set by the door. Using the spray nozzle he cleaned the flagstone of blood and oils, blasting remnants of Pony into the grass. The cutting board he threw away in the trash.

The koi pool was calm. The fish didn't appear to mind their numbers being thinned. Nor did they shy away from him. They didn't understand the role he had played.

It was the heat of the day, normally too hot to be out for long, but Walter felt chilled. He went upstairs and stood for a long time under the steaming water of the shower. Then he sat out on the patio in shorts and bare feet, straining to absorb all the heat the sun could offer. When he closed his eyes, he felt traces of goo and scales on his hands, little bits that hadn't come off in the shower—but when he studied his fingers, nothing was visible.

It wasn't even three o'clock, but Walter poured himself a whiskey. He'd earned it. After the first one he had a second, and by the end of the second a certain calm began to settle on him. He could breathe again. It was the right thing to do and he had done it. By now the fish would be slowing, their eyes dulling. He would leave them in the freezer until garbage day, when he could carry the sacks straight from the makeshift morgue to their waste disposal grave. This was the way to take care of it. It eased their passing.

The image of Sammy and Chloe flashed through Walter's mind, then the face of their father. He took another gulp of whiskey.

A glance at his watch set him in motion. There were things to clean up before Julia got home. He put the knives in the empty dishwasher, and he turned the dial to *sterilize*. He wiped the blood off the slider handle. A new lowball of whiskey in his hand, he picked up the old net and padded barefoot down the hallway to return it to the workbench.

Stepping into the dark garage, he gasped, dropping his cocktail. The glass smashed, sending shards and whiskey over his bare feet.

There, in the middle of the cement floor, lay a long, finned figure, ghostly white. It was Gandalf. The great fish flicked his tail, slapping it against the concrete. His eyes gleamed in the low light, and his lips still opened and closed, as if he were trying to speak. *Wa... wa...* he seemed to mouth. *Water*, of course.

Unless it was something else, something nearly the same, a beckoning, a name.

As Walter's eyes adjusted to the dimness, he saw the others—Orange Juice, Graybeard, Blacky, and more—all of them scattered across the cement as if a storm had passed through, hailing down koi. The door of the freezer stood ajar, the necks of the bags unraveled. They'd sprung themselves free.

A great energy surged inside of Walter, and he roared at the fish, a long guttural roar of frustration. What did they want from him? Couldn't they see there wasn't a thing he could do?

Fast—faster than he had moved in a very long time—Walter stormed to the freezer and grabbed at the bags the fish had left behind. He stuffed koi in, one after the other. Gandalf the ringleader went last. That one, the one who refused to back down, Walter rolled into a separate sack, all by himself. He packed them in the freezer, slammed the door closed. From the workbench he grabbed a roll of duct tape, fumbling to get an edge started, then wrapped a band around the freezer door, reaching it all the way around the back, one layer, then two, then three. He tore off long strips, sealing the door at the top and the bottom, binding it on the sides, not stopping until the roll was empty.

Back in the house he found that his feet were bleeding. With tweezers he plucked shards of glass from his soles, covering the red cuts with Band-Aids from the medicine cabinet. He mopped up the floor. Then he climbed up the stairs and dropped into the bedroom armchair, gazing out the window while his feet throbbed. He didn't move until Julia came home.

That evening he made pasta with a vegetarian sauce. He set the table indoors, protesting that it was too hot to eat out back. Julia asked for a beer, but Walter convinced her to have wine instead.

He was at the sink, draining the pasta in the colander, when she asked the question.

"So," she said as she hunted for the Parmesan in the fridge, her back to him. "Did you do it? Did you take care of it?"

He nodded. Steam rose from the mass of noodles before him, leaving a halo of mist on the windowpane. Out there by the ash tree sat the patio table, not far from the steel barbecue and the patch of blooming yarrow. Further to the left was the stone lip of the koi pond, the surface of the water still, except for the bubbles by the filter.

What bothered him more than the killing was the parting, the leave-taking. Harder to sever than flesh were all those other filaments, the invisible ties that bound him like live nerves to those he loved. He looked around from the sink. At the table Julia scrubbed a block of hard cheese against the grater. He wouldn't tell her now. Not tonight. Tomorrow morning he'd make a call or two and get a reservation. By noon on Saturday the wheels would lift from the tarmac and he'd be rising over the mountains, headed for the plains, for the crisp cold, for the snow, for Peter and Sammy and Chloe, escaping, however briefly, from this warm land with its bubbling ponds and its lies of eternal summer.

THRIFT

WHILE THE SALES GIRL knelt to return the tray of watches to the case behind the counter, Judith slipped a gold necklace off the stand, fingered its textured links, paused, and trickled the fine chain between the flaps of her Dior handbag. Her lips parted and her face flushed with pleasure, as if someone had touched her lengthily in just the right place.

The salesgirl stood and smoothed her skirt over her hips, her eyes brimming with earnestness. Judith almost felt sorry for the poor thing, so keen to earn her commission. Cute, too, and eager to please. Judith liked that about her.

"Anything else I can show you, Ma'am?"

"Not today." Judith left a pause. "I might consider that diamond one, but I'll need to speak to my husband." Husbands could be so useful, in a way. "Why don't you give me your card, dear?"

As Judith walked away, she felt the salesgirl's eyes on her back, and she added a touch of sway to her step.

Such a game this was! The department stores held no secrets. The cameras and mirrors insulted one's intelligence. And store detectives? Please.

Once you knew the layout, it was simple to screen your gestures. Some areas had almost no surveillance. But what was the point of stealing socks and panties? No, the fun came from brushing up against the limit, making valuables disappear like a magician. Distraction and misdirection, that's what you used. Not to mention the mask of expectations: who'd think that a woman like Judith— who was, after all, someone—would do a thing like this? She hardly needed to sneak.

Down the lingerie aisle Judith spotted an olive-skinned girl in a black knit dress. She was handling a red lace teddy—and had the figure for it.

Someone was going to have fun, weren't they? Some grubby man, probably—like Judith's husband, who wasn't just a fiction made up for salesgirls. For better or for worse. She even had a little boy that she'd finally unloaded into the school system. Now her days were her own. At first she'd just tried shopping: hats, shoes, bags, scarves—the whole lot of it. But after a while she'd needed to rub up against something new. She'd wanted a bit of friction.

It began with the fitting rooms. In one of the stores, signs were posted: *This room is monitored by same-sex personnel.* Two-way mirrors was how they did it, of that Judith was certain. There were times she could sense the presence on the other side, and on those occasions she undressed slowly, lingering over buttons and zippers, letting her clothing fall to the floor, turning her hips—all the while her eyes on the mirror, watching herself, but also watching them watch her. And then she would reach back and unclasp the strap, slipping the bra off her shoulders. She would cup her hands under her breasts and lift. It wasn't such a bad sight, was it? Why not give them a little pleasure, too? Sometimes she took off the bottom and stood erect, examining herself in the fitting room mirror. Go ahead and *monitor*.

In housewares Judith traced her fingertip along the rim of a china plate. The olive-skinned girl was there again, over by the display of vases, caressed by that black knit. No denying she was attractive. Their eyes met for an instant, and Judith flashed her the hint of a smile, the acknowledgment of women recrossing paths in a department store. But when the girl's eyes darted away, Judith knew.

All those lustrous curves, wasted on security.

Usually it was men who did this job. Such a clumsy, bumbling lot. Whenever she found them on her tail, she'd lead them around, put on a show of stupid errors, and just when they thought they had her—she could almost feel them getting an erection—she'd slip through their laughable net. Sorry, boys! The best one was last year, uptown, when she dragged that brainless sleuth through a maze of departments after leaving the stolen bracelet inside a sweater she'd considered. At the exit, the brute had clamped his hand on her forearm and dragged her to the manager's office. She gave him the haughtiest look in her stock. When they found nothing on her, the manager dripped with apologies and dressed the fellow down right in front of her. Oh, but she'd relished that—making that man unhand her, taking her pleasure, and not letting him have his.

She paused at the rack of men's ties, trailing the strips of fabric between her fingers. In a slice of mirror she saw that the olive-skinned girl wasn't far behind. A body like that, she could do anything she wanted. And who knows? Perhaps *this* was what she wanted—to watch women like Judith. It was flattering, in a sense. She decided to keep those eyes trained on her a while longer.

As she strolled through the aisles, postponing her departure, Judith prolonged her pleasure. Why rush the moment? In the end, though, they'd both be disappointed. Wouldn't they?

A shiver came upon her. What if she gave the pretty girl what she wanted?

Her heart quickened. She imagined that hand touching her shoulder as she stepped out the door. Judith would struggle a bit—they'd both like that. Those fingers would pick through the intimate packings of her purse. Who knows—maybe she'd be frisked?

Just think what her husband would say.

It would mean risking it all. But wasn't it for this that she'd been waiting? And for such a deliciously long time?

INHERITANCE

PROFANITIES FIZZED on Milo McCrae's lips as he loped down the walk to the shabby garage with the dumpster out front. Half past seven, already! The night sounds of the lake—the loons and the lapping water—had lulled him into a drugged slumber, and he'd woken feeling groggy, fouled by troubled dreams.

Smacking his hands together against the autumn chill, he hoisted the overhead door, and the honeyed light transformed the cans and crates and boat motors and ropes and rake handles into a hoard of gold. For a moment, Milo could have been mistaken for a rich man, a Midas. Then a wisp of cloud slid by and transmuted the garage back into a gray landscape of junk. A mountain range of it. A continent.

There'd be the house to clear out, too.

Up at the cabin the screen door slapped closed, and he tilted his head. No, his sister hadn't started down the walk. Probably Meredith was taking in the view, relishing these last mornings. Maybe she'd at least turned on the coffeemaker. That much was technically possible—though he didn't like to rely on divine intervention.

Charity, charity, he told himself. No need to be a mean-spirited son-of-a-bitch. None of this was her fault. Nor his. *It is what it is.*

Casting a sidelong look into the belly of the garage, he sighed at what it was: chaos in its purest form.

He knew the drill. At work they often gave Milo code to troubleshoot, thousands of lines written by yahoos who couldn't think ahead and didn't know how to document what they'd done. First step was to strip away the clutter. Those functions that were never invoked? Delete them. All the wandering variables? Go on a safari and bring them back alive. Put them in a single holding pen. Give them names that mean something. Only then could you could start to make out what the newbie had intended, after which you could decide if it was salvageable. The garage would be no different.

His eyes fell on the leaky old hip waders hanging from a nail, the ones he used to wriggle into when helping with the dock every spring. Thank God local kids had taken over that ass-freezing job long ago—along with the tongue-lashings that would come whenever they fucked something up. He could imagine his dad growling at some poor teenager who had waded out with a section of dock, and whose testicles were seizing up from the seep of ice water. *Can't you even keep it level?* In hindsight it was almost comical.

But now the dock was history. Not Milo's problem. Before slinging the rubber waders into the dumpster, he turned them upside down and shook. Out tumbled a mummified mouse. Who knew what else might be tucked inside these remnants? He checked the pockets of ratty clothing before hauling it out by the armload, bidding it good riddance. So long to the runs of mildewed magazines. Bye-bye to the filthy old box fan and the ancient storm windows. Farewell to the lawn mower engine that hadn't so much as cleared its throat in a decade. Those bags of empty tin cans? *Sayonara!* The cracking inner tubes from the seventies? *Arrivederci!* The four cases of crumbling clay pigeons? Fly, babies, fly! He was careful—lifting lids, shaking out tarps, poking through crates—but each box was like a Russian doll, junk containing junk containing junk, leading to an empty center.

After each trip to the dumpster he felt a little lighter, like a man in the gondola of a hot air balloon, cutting away sacks of ballast, soon to go airborne. He started to whistle through his teeth while he worked.

Eventually Meredith came down the walk, dressed in soft jeans and a brown cardigan, her sandy hair pulled back in a ponytail—and, wouldn't you know, carrying a cup of coffee for him after all. Why should that surprise him? Why did he always expect the worst?

"You got off to an early start," she said, offering the mug.

He harrumphed. "I wish. It's practically a mythological labor down here. The hydra of many heads. Or a boulder to roll."

He sipped, and the taste of coffee began to lift the veil of his grogginess.

"I was watching you from the porch," she said. "What were you looking for?"

He gave her a baffled look.

"I saw how you were picking through the boxes," she added.

He snorted. He wasn't *picking through* anything. "Just checking. Paints and poisons, you know. I guess there'll be no shortage of the latter."

Her face tightened. "You don't have to talk like that."

"What's the matter?" he said. "No speaking ill of the dead?"

She turned away and Milo rolled his eyes. Oh great. Joking evidently wasn't allowed on these hallowed grounds. But if you want to build a shrine, you really shouldn't do it in a minefield.

After a few more gulps of coffee, he returned to the garage, to the slaughter of innocents. Tomato cages and garden hoses and lumber scraps—out with it all! Tabula rasa, that's what he wanted. It was the Pol Pot method of cleaning. Quick. Thorough. No survivors.

How amusing that she'd thought he was searching for something. No, his goal was emptiness, after which he could head back home with Tommy. He checked his watch: past eight, and the boy was still in bed.

In the garage Meredith started a rearguard action, slipping through the jungle of grade-A debris and rescuing the lucky few from annihilation. First came two pottery vases, next a carton of toys, then a stack of china from some previous generation. She deposited these and other escapees in a growing refugee camp at the edge of the driveway.

When Milo lugged out a box of rusting Tonka Toys—dump trucks, front-end loaders, a steam shovel—she barred his path.

"You're not throwing those out?" It was barely a question.

Indeed he was. These had been his trucks, refuse from his childhood, and he could throw them away if he wanted.

"But what about Tommy?"

His neck went hot. There were so many ways in which this was not her business. He'd promised himself to be patient, but that didn't mean he shouldn't be firm. "It's junk," he said flatly. "And it's mine."

He felt everything sour as Meredith put her hands on her hips. Oh, God, he thought, it was going to be the whole damn spiel, the same as always. He could practically write a program for it: she would make some insinuation, he'd fire back a retort, she'd take offense—and soon they'd be off in a spiraling routine that multiplied the variables of their tempers, like a single-threaded virus that couldn't be interrupted until it consumed the whole processor and crashed the system. It wasn't even about the trucks—not at all—but if she wanted to make it about the trucks, he could play that game. After thirty-eight years of practice, he was a goddamned master at it.

He was honing the barbs of his opening quip when he sensed a presence, turning to find a moon-faced boy with a skinny neck and bright eyes standing behind him.

"Hey, Kiddo!" Milo sang, forcing a laugh. "You're up." All at once he was ashamed for what he'd been on the brink of saying to Meredith, for what his eight-year-old son would have heard.

Tommy wore light blue shorts and a white T-shirt, tennis shoes but no socks. "Aren't you cold?" Milo asked.

The boy rubbed his eyes with his fists. "Nope."

"Good morning," Meredith called out. She, too, looked relieved by his arrival.

"How'd you sleep?" Milo said.

Tommy looked at the partially disemboweled garage. "What are you guys doing?"

"Just getting a start. Cleaning up." To prove it, Milo scooped a stained canvas tarp into his arms.

Tommy followed, hoisting himself up on the rim of the dumpster, scrabbling against the side with the toes of his tennis shoes in order to raise his chin above the edge. He surveyed this cavern of marvels, then lowered himself back to the ground. He spotted the piles Meredith had accumulated in the driveway, and a soft crease formed in his brow.

"Those are undecided," Meredith told him. "The jury's still out."

"Can I look?"

She glanced at Milo, offering him the chance to veto, but he tipped his head.

"Sure thing," she said. "Go crazy."

Off he scampered, harvesting a pile of gadgets: a battered calculator, a stapler, a tiny set of wrenches. From one carton he retrieved several old comic books from Milo's childhood. A crouched Spider-Man showed on the cover of one, the black mask of Batman on another, and Tommy gripped these treasures with both hands.

Who cared about the trucks now, Milo thought. What an idiot he could be. This wasn't an easy trip for any of them, and he needed to hold it together.

As usual, it was Tommy who helped Milo lighten up, who made him better than his normal self. The little dude looked up to him so much, thought he was practically a superhero from one of those comic books. But like all superheroes, Milo had to watch his step, or else one day Tommy would prance around the corner and catch him out of uniform. The kid would realize that the capes and masks concealed a secret identity, that under all the costumes he was nothing more than a Clark Kent or a Peter Parker. Or worse—a Batman who wouldn't even turn out to be Bruce Wayne, but rather the Joker himself. Milo could do better than that, couldn't he? He needed to do better.

Now the kid held up a chunky object. "What's this, Dad?" he called, wagging it in the air. He brought it over and Milo turned the thing around in his fingers, a cube of dense wood, not much bigger than a building block, painted bluish gray. On four sides the head of a buffalo had been carved into the surface with shaky lines. A homely, amateurish job. From top to bottom a hole had been drilled through. Milo stared at it. Part of some game, perhaps? The buffalo block was vaguely familiar, but he couldn't place it.

"Choose carefully," he told Tommy as he handed it back. "You can't keep everything." He knew you had to be careful. A bauble here and there, and pretty soon you can't shake the souvenirs off, they're all over you, like burrs in a dog's fur.

"Should we have some breakfast?" Meredith called out.

The boy's face brightened. "At the coffee shop?"

Milo dithered. He worried about the time it would take. But he'd promised Tommy they'd go at least once. What the hell, why not today? Might as well get it over with.

He didn't bother to close the garage. Maybe someone would come and steal it all. He could hope.

* * *

Their father's body had been found on a humid Monday morning back in June. Milo had attempted to reach him on Sunday, calling twice and leaving messages. Then he'd taken Tommy to soccer practice, stopping afterwards for pizza, and it wasn't until the next morning that he'd thought to try again. When still there was no answer, he called Meredith, but no, she hadn't heard from him either.

That's when he'd phoned Frank Alcott up at the lake, and Frank ambled next door to check things out, knocking and trying the knob before peering through the laundry room window. Cropped by the doorway at the end of the hall, splayed across the carpet, the bare legs of a man were visible.

Natural causes, they'd said.

It finally happened was the way Milo had announced it to Ellen, calling his wife at work. Time and again his father had played chicken with his health, forgetting to take his meds, ignoring recommendations. He and Meredith could call, but an unanswered phone might mean nothing more than a nap or a trip to the liquor store. Maybe he even screened their calls. Twice while their father lived alone the paramedics had been brought in because a neighbor had found him complaining of chest pains. But still the old buzzard had refused assistance. No nurse stopping by, no emergency button necklace. He insisted on his *independence*. Didn't want to be a *burden*. Demanded to be left *alone*.

Milo knew they couldn't count on the neighbors indefinitely. It was like a randomized function in a computer program: unpredictable but inevitable. That's why it wasn't his fault he'd been eating pizza with his son while his father lay dying in his boxer shorts on the bedroom floor. No, not his responsibility.

Meredith had taken it hard, accusing herself. "There's nothing we could have done," Milo told her again and again, though he didn't quite believe his own words. It all depended on where you drew the line.

And then there was Tommy. "I'll never see Papa again!" the boy had cried out in a strangled voice. Later, from behind his bedroom door, Milo had heard weeping, actual sobs, which had astonished him. Never see him again? Hell, the boy had hardly ever laid eyes on his precious *Papa*, a man who had never sent birthday cards, never called, and owed his fleeting appearances in Tommy's life to Milo and Ellen's rare pilgrimages north so their son could see his grandfather because, after all, wasn't that what a family was supposed to do?

*   *   *

The coffee shop was more than a café. It also served as a gas station, a convenience store, a distributor of hunting and fishing licenses, and a bait shop. Milo led Tommy on the obligatory tour past the vats swarming with minnows and three different kinds of frog. There was a glass-fronted cooler that held night crawlers and leeches in Styrofoam containers. They studied the racks of gleaming lures and spinners, all as mysterious as the goods of a magic shop.

In the café a heavy-set waitress with leathery skin and a smoke-raked voice took their order. She recognized Milo as Dale McCrae's son, and soon she was telling Tommy how his grandfather would come up for breakfast, drinking coffee until noon, sitting *right there*, on *that stool* at the counter, swapping war stories with the regulars.

"So what're you going to do with the place?" she asked.

"Sell it," Milo announced. When he saw she was waiting for an explanation, he drummed one up. "Too much to maintain, you know."

She nodded sympathetically, clicked her pen, moved on to the next table.

It was Tommy who brought it up again.

"Why do we have to sell Papa's cabin?"

"Because we can't keep it," Milo stated, avoiding Meredith's eyes.

"But why?" Tommy pressed.

Milo looked at the ceiling. What was he to say? That his nerves clucked like a Geiger counter anytime he came within fifty miles of that place, and that it nearly made him break into hives? That once anger wicks into the walls of a house, it can never come out? Did he have to tell Tommy the stories, describe the drinking bouts, relate the blows that had rained down on Milo's bent back? And by what shorthand could he explain how both the father and son had used Meredith as an uneasy ally, how the price of her allegiance had been the begrudging acceptance of her affection for the other, and how these feelings extended even across the border of death? Meredith felt actual fondness for that lakefront home, while Milo couldn't abide it. Did he have to enter into the grubby details, telling Tommy how she couldn't afford to buy Milo's half, and how you can't divvy up a house the way you do the silverware?

"It would be too expensive," he said simply. "The taxes alone would be a killer."

"But I *love* the cabin."

He was too weary for this discussion. "I'm afraid that doesn't—"

"But it's *Papa's*," Tommy insisted.

"No it's not," he snapped.

The startle in Tommy's eyes told Milo he'd spoken too sharply. He softened his voice. "All I mean is, that's the way it works. Don't you see? Everything that was Papa's becomes Mer's and mine. From the parents to the children. Only, Mer and I, neither of us needs another home."

He prepared to fend off his sister's correction, but she didn't utter a word. He'd succeeded in bullying the conversation into silence.

To redeem himself a little he drove them back the long way, aiming for the undulating strip of road they called the roller coaster. As he accelerated into the first rise, the bumper sank low to the ground until, at the crest, the suspension bounced their stomachs into a flutter of weightlessness. For a moment the Honda became the Batmobile, and Tommy squealed with delight.

"Not too fast," Meredith murmured, gripping the armrest.

He powered into the next rise, and the next, keeping his eye on his son. The roller coaster road was best when you sat in the back, when you only weighed sixty pounds, when you were eight instead of thirty-eight, when your stomach hadn't been numbed by innumerable stretches of turbulence over O'Hare. All these conditions were met by the grinning boy in the back seat, sitting now in the spot Milo himself used to occupy, their eyes meeting in the rearview mirror.

*   *   *

Milo felt like a cautious intruder at the cabin. His father's life had been posted with No Trespassing signs, and now Milo had squeezed through the fence. Clearing out the garage was like poaching on the estate when the master was away.

Tommy brought him a sandwich at lunchtime, eager to help. But the garage was full of sharp and rusty edges, so Milo sent him back to "lend a hand" to his aunt up at the house. In this way the boy was passed back and forth most of the day, and each time Milo saw him, the kid was cradling more souvenirs in his skinny arms. More ballast.

After dinner they called home. Milo described to Ellen the progress they'd made, and Tommy smacked kisses to his mother over the phone. Afterwards Milo tucked him into the upstairs bedroom, the very room he himself had spent summers in as a boy. He examined Tommy's growing collection of scavenged artifacts: antiquated electronics, playing cards, polished rocks, pocket knives. And that odd blue-gray block of wood with the familiar buffalo head outlines. There was the stack of richly colored Marvel and DC comic books, the superheroes and villains from Milo's past fanned out across the dresser top.

"All this?" he said.

"Can I keep it?" the boy murmured.

Milo's hand clenched. He so needed to be rid of it. But Tommy wants it, he told himself. Be one of the good guys. Be Batman. "Sure," he said. "Why not?"

Back downstairs he and Meredith cracked open an ancient bottle of scotch. They spoke cautiously at first, focusing on the work to be done. With the help of the whiskey, they relaxed, and during a silence Milo rattled his ice cubes absentmindedly.

"Ah," Meredith said with a smile, nodding toward his empty glass. "More tea?"

The reference startled him into a vision of the past: he and his sister, no older than Tommy, sitting on crates in the backyard, playing at houseguests. She had poured him a cup of water from a plastic teapot, and while he drank she taught him to hold out his pinky. The Tonka Toys wouldn't have been far away.

Yes, there had been moments like that.

He looked at her now and managed a smile. "Yes please, dear," he replied. "More tea."

*   *   *

As he brushed his teeth that night, a strange face stared back from the mirror, like some kind of residue in the glass. He ran his fingertips along the tired creases of his eyes, and he stroked the line of his jaw. Even the waitress had noted the resemblance. Sure, it was just the surface, but you had to wonder about what lay beneath the mask.

It was like all those comic book stories Milo had reveled in as a boy. How he'd loved the sagas of secret identities and obscure pasts, heroes whose parents had vanished or were not the people you thought. He'd relished the moral dilemmas and tracked the battles against arch-villains: Superman and Lex Luthor, Spider-Man and the Green Goblin, the Hulk and Thunderbolt. His favorite by far had been Batman—the Caped Crusader—a hero whose power was neither a birthright nor an accident, who had created himself, rising above the tragedy of his youth. It could have gone the other way. Bruce Wayne had always held a special darkness inside, and he might have veered toward evil, but instead he'd decided to stand up for what was right, especially against the Joker, the nemesis with the long-faced sneer.

That night Milo woke with a start, tangled in the sheets, fretful from a knot of dreams he was already forgetting. His watch

showed a quarter to four, and try as he might to conjure up soothing thoughts—he pictured Tommy in bed, abandoned to the night,
his pink arms as limp as fabric, his lips parted—sleep was done with
him, and he was stuck with his thoughts.

Inheritance. It was enough to drain a person. In computer programming the principle was so simple. Properties and attributes
were handed down from one class to another, but you didn't have to
take it all. You could pick and choose. A line of code was all it took.

* * *

The next day he worked in the house, emptying the desk and the
file cabinets, skimming for important documents before condemn-
ing stacks of manila folders. He examined the contents of drawers
before dumping them into the trash.

Meredith came upon him pawing through a sack she'd already
filled, and she broke the sullen silence. "What are you looking for
now?"

"Nothing. Why do you keep asking me that?"

"Because you're always digging around. What're you after?"

"Nothing," he repeated. "But someone has to make sure we
don't throw out the baby with the bathwater. There could be something of value."

"But to you it's all bathwater. You go through every box, but you
haven't set a single thing aside."

He sputtered. This was exasperating. Meredith didn't understand, and after his rough night, he was too tired to explain it to her.
Or to himself.

Tommy spent the day down by the old boathouse. From the
window Milo saw his son choose a flat rock, draw back his bony
elbow and flick it awkwardly, plopping the stone into the blue-green
surface without a trace. So clumsy, he thought. Someone should
give that boy a lesson in skipping.

Soon the kid turned up at the house again, antsy, getting underfoot and pleading with his dad to come out and play. As if Milo
could! No, he was too busy hauling his own father's past out to the
trash where it belonged. Time was short, so when Tommy came

whining, he had to be firm.

While sorting through a box of desk supplies, he laid his hand on a block that turned out to be like the one Tommy had found the previous day. This one was bigger, two or three times the size, but painted the same bluish gray, a larger buffalo head branded on all four sides, the same hole drilled through the top.

What the hell were these things? he wondered. They reminded him of some kind of puzzle. In fact, now that he thought about it, hadn't they actually belonged to him, way back when he was Tommy's age or younger? A smudge flickered on the screen of his memory. He'd painted these blocks himself, hadn't he? He studied the outline of the buffalo head. No, not a toy exactly. It had something to do with the smaller one, he was pretty sure, and there'd been other cubes too.

One more crazy school project, like pinch-pot vases and papier-mâché masks. He had to be careful: if he left this block out, Tommy would scoop it up. Milo dropped it in the trash.

* * *

That night he drained a shot of whiskey alone in his room, followed by a second. The first day had felt easy, like a liberation. But now he was slowing down. Each load to the dumpster weighed twice as much as the last. Worse, the more they emptied it out, the fuller the house felt, filled with echoes and recriminations.

He remembered the arguments, barbed with insults one could never extract. He knew exactly where—against what seam of the lily wallpaper, against what piece of furniture—his father had shoved him just before it came to blows. He recalled the time he'd defied the old man, facing him and taking it. And he remembered Meredith, watching from the door of her own bedroom, her knuckles pressed to her lips.

What stuck with him indelibly, and against so many backdrops, was his father's scowl—that look of disdain, the long sneer. What was Milo supposed to feel now? Mourning? He'd finished with that long ago, back in his teens. Relief? Not even. Sorrow? No.

Instead, what welled up inside of him was the pointless,

impossible emotion of anger. Like a man who knows he's been swindled, deeply conned. He wanted to strike out. But there was nothing left to hit.

In a fog of fatigue and whiskey, Milo yearned for home—his *real* home. He wanted to get back to Ellen, to work. His missed the clarity of computer programs. Their predictability. Their fixability. But he and Meredith had this goddamned cabin to deal with, and he'd have to stick it through one more day.

Bed was what he needed now more than anything else. Sleep. Darkness. Reboot.

* * *

He played hide and seek with his dreams all night, waking frequently to stay beyond their reach. In the morning he breakfasted on coffee and aspirin. To keep Tommy out of his hair he located a crusty fishing rod, and out on the beach he taught the kid to cast, demonstrating how to send the bobber sailing through the air. Luckily for Milo, the fish weren't biting, so he wouldn't have to waste time ripping out hooks.

He made three trips to the library that day to drop off boxes filled with books. Old paints and cleaners went to the recycle center. His back bowed under the squares of shingles he pulled down from the garage rafters. He checked out the attic and the crawl space, examined all the high shelves in the closets, disposing of the last traces. Boxes and bags migrated to the driveway, crowding against the over-full belly of the dumpster.

Tommy kept coming in and hounding him for help, not able to get the hang of casting. Milo showed him twice more, but the boy really had no talent for it and made horrible, awkward jerks that sent the line cascading fifteen or twenty feet before it dropped into knee-deep water. Milo gritted his teeth. It wasn't so hard. You just had to put your arm into it. He left Tommy on the beach to practice.

Staggering his way through the final hours, he carted away the slide carrousels and workshop tools, the cleaning supplies and pharmaceuticals. By six o'clock he declared the cabin empty, except for the furniture and their own suitcases.

My God, he thought. Was he finally free? He needed to absorb the enormity of it.

Bone-tired, he rewarded himself with a drink. He'd made it through, hadn't he? He'd survived the long weekend, and soon he'd be out of this house forever. Inside his head the all-clear sounded. He let out a little line, started to breathe.

The whiskey tasted like ambrosia.

"Hey Mer," he called up the stairs. "How about a little celebration?"

Had they really gotten everything out? While he waited for his sister to come down, Milo made one last sweep of the place, checking under the furniture and behind the cushions. Then he pulled the drawers out of the bureau in case something had fallen behind. He lifted up the seat of the piano bench: empty. Inside the light fixtures he found dead bugs. What about the table? Could something be stuck under the top? And what if objects had fallen into the air vents? He poked and pried and nudged.

"What in God's name are you doing?"

It was Meredith, halfway down the stairs, and he felt himself go red.

"Just making sure we haven't left anything behind."

"Milo, please tell me what it is you've been looking for."

"Nothing. Let it go."

She came down the last steps, glaring as though she'd walked in on a thief.

"How stupid do you think I am?" she said. "I've seen you. Every single day. You sift through it all. Every last drawer and box. What are you after?"

"Don't be ridiculous, Mer." His ripe mood was spoiling. Woozy from fatigue and scotch, he had no patience for games.

"Tell me," she pressed. "Please tell me what it is you're looking for."

A blackness began to seep into his mind, a bile of anger. He'd meant it: he wasn't looking for anything.

But how did that square with the evidence? She was right. He'd gone through it all, even flipping the pages of paperbacks and dumping out board games. What had he been up to? It wasn't a search, exactly—not the way his computer programs scanned through data to match a query with a result. For Milo had no specific query. What he wanted eluded even his own imagination. Something impossible. A magic key. A letter. A secret decoder ring. The kind of mystical object that existed only in comic books—one that would help him decipher the past and figure out how everything had gone so wrong. At the very least, if he came out empty-handed, he'd have left no stone unturned, he'd have given the old man every chance. Which would serve to justify his righteous anger.

"It doesn't have to be this way, Milo," his sister said. "It's not too late."

"Fuck it, Mer." He wasn't going to talk. He didn't need her mediating with a dead man. Besides, it didn't matter, because she was wrong: everything was too late, too goddamn late, and that wasn't going to change, especially now, when he could barely keep his eyes open from fatigue.

He knew better than to expect her to take his side. It was the creaks and groans of old antagonisms, the springs of bitterness now tightening and the cogs starting to turn.

"Milo," she murmured.

Why did she keep pressing! He wasn't going to fall for that ploy of tenderness, not again. He started across the room.

"Milo!" she called to his back, but he refused to hear.

Then, just outside the sliding door, the boy appeared, yet again, unable to take care of himself for five fucking minutes, running up onto the deck with his fishing pole, something dark and flat dancing at the end of the line.

"I got one! I got one!" Tommy called, his voice muffled by the glass. "Dad!" he said, followed by words Milo couldn't understand. "Dad! Dad!"

Meredith called his name, Tommy yelled with excitement, and the anger-stained walls had started their murmuring. Milo just wanted to get away. Why the hell was he still locked in this goddamn cabin, filled with so many voices?

"Dad!" he heard again through the glass. "Dad!"

He was sick to death of this whining little pest.

"Dad!"

"Stop it!" he roared at the glass door. "Leave me alone!"

On the other side of the slider, Tommy stumbled backwards, his face cringing in a mixture of surprise and—was it? Yes, it was—fear. An expression Milo recognized. Then, faintly reflected in the glass he saw another face he remembered, one he hadn't seen for a long time. Those eyes. That nose. Those teeth in that mouth. He stepped away from the glass, and the narrow sneering face backed away too. The face of the Joker.

He took the stairs three by three, Meredith hard on his heels, and he ducked into Tommy's room, slamming the door behind him.

On the bed, he cradled his head in his hands. That face, it had crept up on him, appearing just when he thought he was safe. There was no escaping it, no way to cast it off into the dumpster with the rest. It was inside, part of Milo himself, and Tommy had seen it.

Innocent Tommy—both witness and heir apparent.

Across the dresser top were all the horrible souvenirs the boy had collected, the old office supplies and shells and polished stones, the comic books. Once again Milo laid his eyes on the blue-gray cube, the one with the crudely carved buffalo heads.

It was the damnedest thing, that block. Where the hell had it come from? How did it fit with the other one? And why in God's name would anyone have kept such trash—junk like everything else in this cabin, where over the course of thirty years, *nothing had changed*, where he hadn't even wanted to return to clear it out. But their father had had the last laugh, hadn't he, tricking them into coming up here again? Except that now Milo had become the father, had come here with his own son, and had now started his own reign of terror. The little one had become the big one.

He looked again at the blue-gray cube on the dresser, and all at once he remembered. The big one and the little one. No, not a toy, not a puzzle. It was Little Buffalo. From that scouting group, the one for kids, the name of which escaped him. How old had he been? Seven or eight? At the workbench in the basement of the old house he'd gotten to hold the handsaw, learning to pull and not to push. Then had come the sanding, lots of it—what had seemed like hours of stroking the wood with coarse paper, then fine and finer. The memory of a smell, like a fireplace, but different. A large hand had guided Milo's as he traced the outline of buffalo heads with a wood-burning pen, first on one block and then the other. The same fingers had showed him how to apply the paint.

That was what he remembered the most: the feeling of his father's hands cupped around his own, sweeping the brush across the surface.

The blocks, they were used at the meetings with the other fathers and sons. As they arrived they would slide these animal heads down a metal rod, adding them in a kind of ritual, one block for the father and one for the son, each big animal accompanied by a small one, all of them stacked into a totem pole. A little silly, yes, but also a little sacred.

And his father had saved these?

When Milo emerged from the bedroom, it felt like hours had passed, but no, the sun wasn't even fully set, and Tommy still waited on the deck, shivering in his shorts, dunking the hooked sunfish into a pail of water to keep him alive. Milo greeted his son with an apology. Not tonight, but soon, they would talk. For now he took care of the fish.

Of course the hook was all the way down the gullet. He fetched the green metal tackle box from the boathouse and found a pair of needle-nosed pliers, teaching Tommy how to extract the barb without pulling the insides out. They slid the sunny into the pail so Tommy could watch it swim, and only the slightest hint of pink emerged from its gills.

"Look at it go," Tommy said. "Look at it!"

Milo rested his hand on the boy's shoulder. "Yes," he said. "I'm looking."

*　　*　　*

Later, after he and Meredith patched up their alliance, Milo pulled his shoes back on and rummaged in a box for a flashlight. The screen door slapped closed behind him and he followed the beam over the cracked sidewalk down to the dumpster. There was no need to hurry, and probably it didn't make sense. After all, mostly it was clutter, like the unused functions in programs he reviewed, variables that had gone crazy, or code that couldn't be salvaged.

There was no magic key, no Rosetta Stone. But at least he'd understood that it wasn't all or nothing. You really could pick and choose, taking only what was worth saving. The sorting wouldn't be easy, but easy wasn't always what mattered.

For now, he wanted to lay his hands on a few of the old objects. To touch them. Maybe those ancient hip waders. A carrousel of slides. But most of all, Big Buffalo, wherever he was, rolling around in the bin.

That would be a start.

FUTURE
PERFECT

BY THE TIME YOU READ THIS LETTER I will be dead.

I'm only fifteen years old, but don't beat yourself up over it. Even though it's your own damn fault.

You are thirty. And mostly I fear you will have disappointed me.

Tell me: Do you recall the name of the turtle that escaped from its tank and ended with its head squished in the screen door?

What about playing freeze tag with Mick and Kelsey and Emily, that time up at the cabin?

How about all those garter snakes, the ones we kept in the garage in a plastic tub until they escaped?

Do you remember *anything*?

What about later? Like the boy at camp, the one who wanted to share a sleeping bag, and then pressed himself against you that way? Do you remember lying in the grass at night at the base of the water tower with Jennifer M., placing your mouth on hers while your hand slipped beneath her shirt? Do you have any recollection of the violence of my desires?

Do you remember your promises? How you would never betray anyone? How you would travel the world? How you would learn six languages? How you would never vote? How you would always be your own boss? How you would never, ever become like your father?

By the time you read this, you will no longer be me. Just a copy of a copy of a copy. There may be some resemblance, but it won't go very far—no more than I can recognize myself in that other boy, the one who bore my name and lived at my address half a lifetime ago, when he was seven or eight.

I am writing this letter in Mrs. Grant's AP English class. The school will mail it to you fifteen years from now. This is not the version I turned in for a grade. This one is for you. To remind you of what you have forgotten. Even though I know it's too late.

I am afraid of what, at the time you read this, will already have taken place. I can feel the seeds of disappointment sprouting inside me even now.

I had hoped for better.

Let me give you a bit of advice. An assignment, really. Sit down and write a letter to the you that you'll have become when you've doubled your age yet again. Include this one with it, to remind our future self of what you will have used to want.

Make him listen to both of us. Because, you see, you're the only chance I have.

Do it now. I don't trust you to wait. It doesn't have to be long. Choose a good address. And don't forget the proper postage.

THIS
JEALOUS
EARTH

THE WORLD WAS SLATED to end in just under two hours, and from her perch on the kitchen stool—her pink-striped tennies barely reaching the lower rung—Cat watched her big brother rummage through the pantry. Randy's jeans sagged low around his butt, barely hanging on, like a rock climber losing his grip. The back of his T-shirt sported the letters WTF in bold capitals followed by a question mark. Muttering in a stage whisper, he reached through the standing army of soup cans, retrieving first a bag of rice, then a jar of flour, a canister of oatmeal, a Ziploc pouch filled with dark brown seeds, and last of all two packages of Jell-O: one lime, one mixed fruit. He shook his head.

Their mother labored at the aluminum sink, scrubbing with a Brillo. Lines of muscle showed in Sheila's arms, and the cross on her necklace swung back and forth as she scoured.

"There aren't even any *crackers*," Randy said, separating out each word. When his mother didn't respond, he allowed himself one more syllable: "Jeez."

Cat cringed.

"Watch your mouth," Sheila said without lifting her head from the basin.

"All I said was *jeez*."

"It's the name of the Lord, Randy, and you know it."

Cat saw the curl form on her brother's upper lip. She shrank inside. *Don't do it. Don't say anything.* Her bare ankles tightened around the legs of the stool.

Maybe Randy got the message. He ran his tongue over his lips. First the top, then the bottom. He gave his head a wag, then turned away and yanked open the refrigerator.

Cat clutched Mr. Tubs against her chest. The rabbit's glass eyes were dull, he suffered from a touch of mange, and his ears had been well-chewed over the years. Somehow he'd leaked bits of his innards and gone rather flat. Cat—Catherine Ann—was eleven, too old for stuffed animals, but today of all days she needed Mr. Tubs.

"There's absolutely nothing to eat in here," Randy moaned as he peered into the fridge. "This is *fucking* ridiculous."

Their mother shuddered at the use of the F-word, but continued to round crumbs on the countertop into her hand.

"Hello?" Randy crooned as if entering an empty house. "Is anyone even listening? Hel-*lo*?"

Sheila's shoulders tightened.

Cat whispered, "I have some Gummi Bears in my room."

Randy shot her a dark look. "*Mom*?" he said.

Sheila puffed strands of hair from her face and turned around. She stood nearly a head shorter than Randy, who at sixteen was bigger than most of the other high-school boys. Cat thought there was something brave about her mom's pose, the way her hands braced her hips as she held Randy's glare, not backing down.

"I don't know what you're expecting," she said. "It's not like I'm going to the grocery store, you know. I'm done going to the grocery store, Randy. Finished."

"That's great," he said. "I'm really happy for you. But what about me? What am I supposed to eat?" He left an opening for an answer, but none came. "How about leaving me a few bucks? A credit card, maybe? You're not gonna need it, right?"

Cat closed her eyes. *Don't say it.*

But of course he did say it. "Since your pal Jesus is coming by, maybe He could perform a little magic for us. You know—produce a few Wheat Thins or something."

Sheila thudded the Brillo into the sink. "Don't talk like that."

"Why not?" Randy snorted. "What more can He do to me?"

She glowered, her jaw clenched. Cat couldn't tell if she was going to scream with anger or melt into tears. Then her mother broke away, strode to the phone desk and dug the billfold out of her purse, landing it on the countertop like a slab of meat. When she spoke, her voice quavered. "Take the whole thing, Randy. The checkbook too."

Then she performed what Cat considered the most amazing gesture of all. She stepped forward and raised her arm—Randy flinching as though she might strike him—and laid a hand on her son's shoulder. She went up on her tiptoes and planted a kiss on his forehead. A miracle.

"It's not too late," she whispered.

Even Randy was thrown off-balance. Their mother was halfway out the kitchen before he bounced back and fired off his next zinger. "What about the car?" he called. "Can I use the car, too, while you're gone?"

There was a hiccup in Sheila's stride, but she didn't stop, and Cat thought she heard the beginning of a sob.

Facing the empty door, Randy began to deflate. His shoulders sagged and his fists opened into soft hands.

"Randy," Cat murmured, making him wheel around.

His chest swelled again. "What are you staring at, Kiddo?"

She tightened her hold on Mr. Tubs. "I don't like this," she murmured.

"Don't you worry, Kitty Cat." He swaggered over. "You see what Mom just did? That's what you call turning the other cheek. You'll hear a lot about that on your little trip." He patted her on the head before turning away. In the doorway he brandished the billfold. "Gonna order me a pizza."

Alone now, Cat tried to breathe. She closed her eyes, and inside her head the hymn was playing:

> He's coming soon, He's coming soon;
> With joy we welcome His returning;
> It may be morn, it may be night or noon—
> We know He's coming soon.

Even though it was a Saturday, they'd sung it just a few hours before, during the special service they'd had at their church, the one that used to be the dry cleaner's. She pictured Mom singing and clapping, her eyes closed, her body swaying, all relaxed for once.

Even Dad was there, not good at keeping the beat, but singing along all the same. Only Randy refused to go.

At the service today, Reverend Willis had reminded them to be prepared. *For today is the day!* he'd bellowed.

All those weeks ago, when her parents first told her, it had sounded like a fairy tale: kind of scary at the same time it was kind of nice. But not real. No, definitely not real.

Then she saw a headline in the newspaper. An important man out in California had predicted it all, right down to the minute. Reverend Willis kept bringing it up in his sermons, adding images from the Bible. She could picture the four horsemen, and even the seven trumpeters. But what about the scorpion-tailed locusts or the Angel of Woe? The Beast of the Sea didn't sound nice at all. Worst of all was the lamb with seven horns and seven eyes. Whenever she tried to imagine that one, it gave her the shivers.

Kids had started talking at school, mostly in whispers though, because not everyone was going to be saved, and Cat didn't want to hurt their feelings. Bit by bit, as the days passed, the fairy tale had started to sound real, like a scary picture in a book that begins to move and get bigger and bigger and make noise, until one day you find that you're inside it. And by then it's too late.

Even worse, Mom and Dad had sat down with Cat three nights ago, wiping tears from their eyes. Randy, they explained, would not be coming with the rest of the family. It was Reverend Willis who had told them. He would be left behind. Randy had sinned, and he refused to ask for forgiveness.

Left behind? Cat had sat in her room that evening repeating those words, her hamster Rascal pressed to her chest. Her brother had always been difficult, especially with Mom. All those screaming matches! Cat never understood why they couldn't get along. But *left behind?*

Mom had sobbed in her bedroom, the door closed.

Randy had laughed out loud when Cat asked him about it. An angry laugh. It was all *bullshit*, he'd said.

But what even happened to those who didn't go? Nobody wanted to stay behind. Even Grandma and Grandpa would be coming—

The dead in Christ who 'neath us lie; In countless numbers, all shall rise. She didn't know what it would be like for Randy. She didn't even want to think about it.

She opened her eyes now to find herself still in the spotless kitchen. According to the red plastic clock above the sink—the one Mom had set to the second so that they would know exactly—it was nearly five o'clock. Hardly an hour left. *He's coming soon, He's coming soon.*

She climbed off the stool and carried Mr. Tubs down the hallway to her parents' bedroom to find her father.

Ordinarily her dad would be out in his wood shop on a Saturday, dressed in jeans, fixing something or making Adirondack chairs for another church sale. But today Cat found him in his bedroom, wearing a crisp white shirt and dark slacks. When she arrived, George was staring at two socks drawn from the mound of laundry heaped on the bed, trying to see if they matched. Behind him, from the corner shelf, a plaster Virgin Mary cast a compassionate look on his work. George's hands were shaky, and he fumbled as he bound the socks together. Next he turned to the T-shirts, laying each one on the bed face down, and folding it with care, first the left side, then the right, then in half, then flipping it over and adding it to the stack.

"Daddy," Cat said. "Don't we need suitcases?"

Her father stopped folding and straightened up. There were dark crescents under his eyes. "No, honey. Where we're going you won't need clothing." He wiped his forehead with the back of his hand and returned to the folding business.

Won't need clothing? Cat's pulse quickened. She considered asking for more details, but didn't dare, terrified of what her father might say. She drew the stuffed rabbit against her chest. With his long ears she could cover herself if she had to.

"Can I at least bring Mr. Tubs?"

Her father stopped again. When he spoke, his voice sounded tired. "Yes, Kitten, I think you can bring Mr. Tubs."

"And what about Rascal?" she blurted, astonished not to have thought of her hamster's fate before now.

"I don't know, honey. No. I don't think so."

She felt a surge of panic. Where could she turn? Randy couldn't help: he was too allergic. But it wasn't fair. Rascal hadn't done anything wrong.

"Please, Daddy?"

He sighed. "You'll have to ask your mother." He started folding another T-shirt, one of hers—her favorite, the one from church camp with a picture of a lamb on it.

So much would be left behind! Cat lowered her voice to a whisper. "Daddy, what's going to happen to Randy?"

Her father stared at his feet, his head so low she could see the bald patch on top. "I don't know, dear," he replied softly. After a moment he reached for another shirt.

They were never ever going to see Randy again, and Dad just kept folding the laundry—Dad, who never folded the laundry. And Randy? He was in his room playing a video game.

In the hallway she found her mom thrusting the vacuum back and forth, as though trying to plane the carpet right off the hardwood. There were dark smudges of mascara on her cheeks. Cat waved with both hands until she caught her mother's attention. Sheila powered the machine down.

"Why are you vacuuming, Mom? I mean, if we're not coming back?"

Sheila wiped at her cheek with the heel of her hand. "Well," she said, her voice cracking, "I'm not leaving the place like *this*." She gestured to display the evidence.

Like what? Cat examined the hallway. It looked fine to her. But vacuuming was what her mom did when she was upset.

"Daddy said I should ask you about Rascal."

Sheila squinted as if Cat were speaking a foreign language.

"*Rascal*. I mean, can I bring him with?"

"Honey, no." She gave a pained look. "Rascal is a hamster. You can't bring him with."

Cat's stomach tightened. "But what will happen to him?"

Sheila didn't answer. She'd gone pale, had closed her eyes.

"Mom?" Cat said, trying to jiggle her attention back.

"I don't know, dear." Her voice was high. "I just don't know.

And I can't think about it right now." She pushed the button and the Hoover motor swelled to a roar.

"Cat!" Randy yelled from his bedroom. "Your phone's ringing."

But she didn't go to answer it. Instead she slipped into Randy's room—usually forbidden territory—dragging Mr. Tubs by the ear. Music posters from bands Cat didn't like pocked the wall like artillery blasts. It smelled of dirty laundry. Randy sat hunched at the computer desk, his cell phone pressed to his head.

"Pepperoni," he was saying. "And onions. Do you have breadsticks?" He paused. "Uh-huh. Yeah, delivery...."

After concluding his transaction, he turned to face his sister.

"Aren't you worried?" she whispered. "About what's going to happen?"

He leaned forward. "Remember what I told you? Nothing's going to happen."

For the first time, Cat felt her lip tremble. "I don't like this," she said. "I want to be with you."

Randy looked away and massaged his forehead with his fingertips. "It'll be fine, Kitty Cat. You just wait. Tomorrow morning we'll be sitting in the living room reading the funnies."

"That's not what Mom says."

"Mom's insane. So is Dad. And they're wrong about a lot of shit." He forced a laugh. "Remember Santa Claus? The Tooth Fairy?"

Cat lowered her voice. "Some of the kids at school," she said, "they're going, too."

"They think they're going," he corrected her.

"How come you can't you come with us, Randy?"

"You mean, if you really were going somewhere?"

She folded her arms and waited.

Randy gritted his teeth. "Stuff I did."

"What stuff?"

"All sorts of stuff. Disrespecting my elders, for one—like Reverend what's-his-face at the dry cleaner's."

Yes, Cat remembered the chalk dust Randy had sprinkled all over Reverend Willis's chair on the altar, which left two white blobs on the back of his robes when he stood. Even the grown-ups had tittered.

"Not coming to church," Randy continued. "Taking the Lord's name in vain." He accompanied this with a roll of his eyes.

"In vain?" Cat said.

"You know. God fucking damn, and all that."

Was that all it took? She studied Randy, uncertain.

"All right," he said. "You wanna know what *really* pissed off the Reverend? You wanna know the Big One?" He leaned even closer, his nose nearly touching hers. "*I don't believe.*"

It took her a moment to understand. Then confusion yielded to relief. It could be so easy! "But Randy," she nodded. "Don't you see? Do it. Just for now."

He raised his palms in defense. "Sorry, Kitty Cat. You either got it or you don't."

"Mom says you just have to say you're sorry, that God will forgive you."

His expression darkened. "I'm not going to lie about it, if that's what you mean."

A cleft formed in her brow. Randy lied about everything. Why not this?

He turned back to his computer.

There was so much she needed to say to her brother, now, before it was too late. She wanted to tell him to knock it off, to stop pretending to be so brave. She wanted him to understand how scared she was. Most of all she wanted to tell him how much she loved him, saying it in a way that wouldn't make him tease her. But she couldn't find the words for any of this, so instead she asked about the hamster. "What's going to happen to Rascal?"

Randy made a crack about the fluff-ball of allergens living in her bedroom. He gestured to the window, suggesting where hamsters might roam free. When he turned back to Cat, his smirk dissolved all at once. "Hey! Hey!" he said, looking as though she were a vase that had just slipped from his fingers and shattered on the floor. "Don't cry, Kitty Cat."

"I'm not crying," she protested as a tear dribbled down her cheek.

Randy turned to his desk, sinking his head between his fists. "I'm sorry, Cat." He rocked forward. "I can't help you. Hell, I can't even help a goddamn hamster." His breathing came in grunts, sounding almost like hers. "And Mom," he said, his voice warbling. "She doesn't even care."

Cat felt something crumble inside of her. Had she ever, ever seen Randy cry? Here was the Angel of Woe in person, right next to her. She hesitated, then reached out and let her fingertips rest on her brother's back. His chest heaved. If only he would say he was sorry!

Their mother's voice from down the hallway split them apart: "Catherine Ann! Where are you? It's time to put on your dress!"

"Look," Randy murmured, still not facing her. "I don't know what to do about Rascal. I really don't. Let me think about it."

Cat padded out of Randy's room and wiped her eyes before disappearing into her own, shutting the door tight. The little pine dresser stood primly by the window, and the green curtains opened out onto the back yard. Her Sunday dress, a bell of white, waited on the bed.

Why couldn't she just wear jeans?

Her cell phone was blinking. It was a message from Serena, a rambling monologue, kind of a farewell, just in case it was true, in case they never saw each other again. After the message ended the voicemail lady gave the options, and Cat pressed three. At least something from this world would be saved.

So now it was goodbye? So it really was real? All the teachers at school had refused to discuss it, and during the last week everyone had kept doing gym and music and math, every single day, as if the most important thing of all was for kids to master their multiplication tables before they got raptured up into the sky or blown to smithereens. But supposedly it was all for the best?

> In these, the closing days of time,
> What joy the glorious hope affords!

She tried to feel the joy.

Because Cat was mostly an obedient girl—though not so

obedient as everyone seemed to think—she pulled on her white dress and checked it out in the mirror. With her index finger she prodded her chest. Some girls in the sixth grade were already getting boobies, but not her. She was so scrawny she had to keep pulling the white straps back up over her shoulders.

The wicker basket on her floor teemed with stuffed animals: the teddies, the toucan, the monkeys. She made sure to touch each one. There was the crucifix on the wall over her bed, the one with the sad but kind-looking Jesus. He wouldn't hurt Randy, would he—Jesus the lamb?

Then the image from the sermons loomed in her mind: the lamb with seven horns and seven eyes. A monster. She shuddered.

Her gaze fell on the bookshelf. Oh, those books! *The Secret Garden, Black Beauty, A Wrinkle in Time*. Would she really never see them again? And there was Rascal, down in his little prison, rolled into a ball in his wood shavings. She clicked open the door and pulled him out, his pink nose quivering over the palm of her hand, the whiskers tickling. She caressed his fur with her cheek and took a deep breath to help hold back the tears. Poor Rascal.

After returning him to his cage, she poured pellets into the food tray and filled his bottle with fresh water.

She had a thin pocket in her dress, a little one where Mom told her to always keep a Kleenex. At first she allowed herself a single picture of Randy, but after that it was hard to stop. In went the tiny carved horse, the blue-green agate, her silver ring, the multi-colored eraser, a rubber ball, the half-eaten package of Gummi Bears. Some paper clips, a pad of post-its. Room was getting scarce. She folded in the four dollar bills that lay on her desk. A pen. That could be handy. And her cell phone, because who knew for sure? Her pocket felt heavy now. It weighed her down. This jealous earth didn't want to let her go.

She still had Mr. Tubs. Dad had promised she could bring Mr. Tubs.

The clock in the kitchen showed 5:27 and it was supposed to happen at 6:00, but Cat felt a terrible hunger. Mom was making a racket in the hall closet, and Dad had disappeared again. She dragged Mr. Tubs back to the kitchen, opened the pantry and began to rummage. Randy was right: there was hardly a thing to eat. In the end she dug out a heel of bread from the bottom of a bag and made herself a mustard sandwich, squirting the yellow sauce on thick. It left an unpleasant aftertaste, even after two glasses of water, and still she was hungry.

From the sink window she watched Mr. Reid from next door walking Thor, his wiener dog, around the fence at the corner. Thor's tail whipped back and forth as he sniffed at the shrubbery.

The last time she'd ever see Thor again. Or Mr. Reid.

"Cat!" Randy called from his room. "Cat! I've found something. For Rascal."

She charged down the hallway. Her brother was at his computer, and when he looked up, she saw red around his eyes.

"Look at this," he said, pointing at the screen. "I found a place that'll look after him. Not that anyone's going to need to," he added. "But still."

She threw her arms around Randy's neck and tried to follow his explanation. But she was so nervous she couldn't concentrate, so she tore down the hall and fetched Dad, dragging him into Randy's room. He peered at the screen. "I don't get it," he said. "What does it do?"

Randy explained. "They take care of your pet if you get raptured."

Cat gritted her teeth with hope. "Can we do it, Dad? For Rascal?"

He tried to skim the page without his bifocals. "My goodness! Two hundred dollars?"

"What does it matter, Dad?" Randy said. "You're not taking the money with you."

He rocked his head back and forth. "I know, but still...."

"I'll pay for it," Randy continued. "Mom already gave me the checkbook. And the credit card."

"She did what?"

"I can sign him up for it myself."

"Please, Daddy," said Cat.

"Two hundred dollars? For a hamster?"

When their mother came in, everyone was talking at once. Cat called to her, waving her forward. But Sheila wasn't interested in the computer. Her eyes were focused on the middle of Cat's body.

"Catherine Ann Driscoll," she cried. "What have you gotten on your dress?"

And when Cat looked down, she found that she had indeed gotten something on her dress—a bright yellow spot, smack dab in the middle of her lap. Something that looked like mustard.

"Come on," her mother growled as she dragged her off to the kitchen, glancing up at the clock. She took a wet sponge and dabbed at the stain. The tactic succeeded in diluting the mustard, and the only thing for it was more water and more dabbing, until Cat was left with a vast wet spot spreading down toward her knees, tinted with the faintest hint of yellow.

"Mom!" wailed Cat, "I can't go like this!"

"And what's all this stuff in your pocket?" Sheila plucked out the cell phone, the dollars, the pen. When she came to the picture of Randy, her breath caught.

Cat looked up at the red clock on the wall. "Mom," she said, "You have to help me."

"Yes," she replied, forcing the words out. "Yes, of course." She let Cat lead her into the bedroom where the others were waiting.

"Quick," Cat said, pointing at the computer. "It's for Rascal."

"What's for Rascal?" she mumbled, her eyes locked on her son.

"This!" Cat tapped on the computer monitor.

"Hey! Don't touch the screen," said Randy. "It leaves smears."

As Sheila read, the energy drained from her body. "This is about pets."

"I know!" cried Cat. "That's what I said."

"It's run by a bunch of atheists," George added.

"But that's why it works," Randy sputtered. "Don't you see? That's how you know they'll still be here after you get raptured."

Sheila stood up straight. "We can't pay a bunch of atheists."

Randy stood up, holding out his empty hands. "Just because they're atheists doesn't mean they're not trustworthy. Hell, *I'm* an atheist."

Cat winced.

"Don't say that!" Sheila cried.

"But I am!" He turned away. "Though I guess that proves your point, right? I mean, that's why I'm fucked, isn't it?"

"And stop using language like that!"

"Take it easy, everyone," George said, patting the air. "Take it easy."

"Why shouldn't I use language like that?" Randy cried. "After all, that's why I'm stuck here while you all get saved. Not that it seems to bother you very much."

"It's your choice," his mother pleaded. "You can still come! Just tell Him you're sorry, Randy."

"Oh, right! So now I have to talk to your imaginary friend, is that it?"

Sheila clamped her hands over her ears and bolted from the room.

"Is that it?" Randy cried, pursuing her into the hallway. "Is it?"

"Randy!" George called as he followed.

Each shouted word pierced Cat like an arrow. Why wouldn't they stop arguing? Time was so short! She hesitated, then hurried after them. Despite everything, she didn't want to be left alone.

They ended up in the living room, where Sheila turned.

"I didn't tell you to *blaspheme!*" she wailed, wiping her cheeks.

Randy clenched his hands, raising his eyes to the ceiling. "You really think that's going to do it, Mom? All I have to do is say *God damn, God fucking damn*, and that kicks me out of paradise? Is that how it works?"

"Just say you're sorry!" she shrieked. "He'll forgive you!"

"That's bullshit!"

"Randy!" George said. "Don't talk to your mother like that!"

"Say it, Randy!" Sheila cried. "Please! For me, just say it."

"Because if that's how it goes, I don't want any piece of your fucked up heaven."

"Randall!" George commanded.

"Your *shitty* heaven," he bellowed, "with your *fucking* savior."

Cat wheezed deeply, a great gasp between sobs. Everyone turned in her direction, silenced, their bodies slackening as though they'd sprung a leak.

"Stop arguing all the time!" she pleaded. "You're always arguing."

Her father reached out to touch her, but Cat pulled away.

"It's all right, Kitten," he said. "It'll be all right."

"No it won't! It won't be all right!" she cried. "I don't want to do this. I won't leave without Randy. I want him to come with us." She turned to her father. "Daddy? Please?" The tears were streaming now, but she didn't care.

George's shoulders rounded and he shook his head, his mouth open. "I'm sorry, Kitten. It's not up to me."

But who was it up to? Who got to decide? Cat looked around at the members of her family, waiting for someone to do something.

Through the kitchen doorway the clock was visible. "It's almost time," Sheila whispered. "We should go and stand in the yard."

"Why the hell do you have to go outside?" said Randy. "For better reception? Is it like a cell tower thing?"

"Sheila," George said, "what possible difference could it make where we stand?"

"I... I just think...."

"Hey, Jesus," Randy said as he took a step to the left, his hand cupped over his ear. "Can you hear me now?"

"Let's just go," said Sheila.

Cat could hardly breathe. She tried to catch Randy's eye, looking for a sign of what he wanted, deep down.

Her mother stepped toward the door, but Cat didn't budge.

"Come on, Kitten," her dad said.

She shook off her father's hand. Dropping Mr. Tubs to the floor, she made a break for it, lunging forward and throwing her arms around Randy's waist, burying her head in his chest, gripping as hard as she could, making an iron ring of her arms. She wasn't going to let go, no, not for anything.

As Randy recovered from the tackle, he surprised his sister by settling his hands on her back, first tentatively, then more firmly.

Nearly a hug. "Send me a card, Kitty Cat," he whispered into her ear. "Goodbye."

She squeezed him all the harder.

"Hurry up," Sheila said, her voice shaking.

"I'm not going," Cat cried into Randy's chest.

The room went quiet.

"What?" Sheila croaked.

"I'm not going with you."

"Kitten," her father said. "Please."

Sheila drove her index finger toward Randy. "What have you been telling her?"

"Nothing!" he spat back.

"It's not his fault!" Cat cried, her head still plastered against Randy's shirt.

Sheila pulled at the sleeve of her dress. "Let go of him! Let go!" She began to pry Cat's arms free.

Which was when Cat did it.

"Damn," she said in her thinnest voice—so weak she worried it wasn't enough.

Sheila gasped, staggering back.

"God damn," Cat added, just to make sure.

"What are you doing?" Sheila cried. "Take that back!"

"God fucking damn," Cat said, louder.

"Catherine Ann, take it back!"

"She's not taking it back," yelled Randy. "Tell *that* to Reverend Fuckhead!"

Sheila shot a glance at the clock. The second hand was sweeping from the six en route to the twelve. It was time. "George," she whimpered.

But George had frozen, his face stricken, his body slack.

"Goodbye Daddy," Cat said. She reached out to touch him, one last time.

He took her fingers in his and studied them dumbly. Cat watched as his gaze moved from her hand to her wrist, then followed the line of her arm past the elbow, all the way to her shoulder and neck, ever upward. Finally their eyes met, and Cat poured everything she had left into that one look. Her father closed his eyes. He stepped toward her.

"George!" Sheila said again.

"God damn," he murmured. Then, with a hint of assertion, "God fucking damn."

Silence fell over the group. Sheila stood alone, her arms dangling. She reminded Cat of Mr. Tubs after his stuffing leaked away. Even her eyes looked dull and scuffed.

While the second hand marched the final steps toward the top of its arc, Cat stood her ground, locked in an embrace with her brother and father. Even Randy had gritted his teeth.

The second hand crested the twelve. And it continued, ticking its way toward the one, the two, the three. Leisurely, like a wiener dog out for a stroll, it followed its path from number to number, drifting down, then creeping back up on the other side.

Sheila checked her watch.

Then, just as breathing resumed, a bell rang. Not the trumpets of the End of Time, not the knell of humanity, but a simple two-toned chime. The doorbell. All four Driscolls exchanged looks, seeking a pair of eyes that understood the nature of this intervention. How was it supposed to work? No one seemed to know the details. One by one they turned to Sheila, who rotated toward the front door and tilted in the direction of the threshold. She reached for the pearl-colored knob.

"Please, Mommy," Cat whispered.

Sheila's hand stopped. Her fingers shivered, closed into a fist, then loosened again. She glanced back at her family, and Cat saw her head dip to the left and right, as though she were calculating, weighing, reckoning.

"Sheila," said George.

When she leaned again toward the door, it was Randy who spoke. Just one word, his voice cracking. "Mom."

Cat watched as her mother turned and met her son's unblinking gaze. Randy's arm was outstretched. Sheila's lips parted and her brow wrinkled, producing a mournful look that Cat had only ever seen in pictures at church. Then Sheila raised her hand and reached out, cautiously, as though approaching something very hot. Her fingers knit together with Randy's, and she let him draw her into the fold.

"God damn," Sheila breathed.

Wordless, they stood in a huddle as the bell rang again, followed by the sound of knuckles rapping against the wood. Cat didn't know what to expect. She thought of Reverend Ellis, of Serena, of Thor, of Rascal, of the Beast of the Sea and the lamb of seven eyes and seven horns. Whatever happened, she'd be with the ones she loved.

A voice beckoned from the other side—a young man's voice, etched with impatience—and Cat caught a whiff of something new but also familiar. It was an aroma of yeast and oregano, a tangy, comfortable smell that reminded her of evenings in front of the television set, of busy afternoons, of hot summer days and late nights. Of family.

FIELD
NOTES

I WAS ELEVEN THE SUMMER we drove to Arizona, the five of us jittering through fifteen hundred miles in an overloaded Town & Country station wagon with failing air conditioning. At fourteen, Neil was too sullen to complain, but if Willy or I piped up from the back, bleating about our boredom or our bladders, or if Willy rammed his bony elbow into my side, working it like the claw of a crowbar until I cried out, Dad was ready with the usual refrain. "Is it killing you?" he'd call back over his shoulder. He loved to ask if things were death threats, which was the threshold for taking action. And when our silence allowed how it wasn't, he'd follow up with: "Whatever doesn't kill you makes you stronger!"

"Terrific," Mom muttered once into the window while a bead of sweat dribbled down her temple. "Maybe I'll just go for that first option."

During the drive she eyed each passing Holiday Inn with theatrical emphasis: those oases sported restaurants with waitresses and pools with chaises longues. Instead, our fate was a housekeeping cabin in a tourist park at the edge of Sedona, where fifteen or twenty cottages were rounded up like Conestoga wagons. Ours was a two-bedroom model, so full of houseflies that complimentary strips of flypaper had been offered by the management, the way a fancier outfit might place mints on your pillow. That first evening, while Dad drank Grain Belt out on the porch, Mom wrestled open a jar of spaghetti sauce and slopped the contents over a matted mound of boiled noodles. Blackened toast, caked with garlic butter, gave our meal that European je ne sais quoi. After dinner, Neil, Willy and I bolted from the table to play Frisbee and freeze tag with the other kids, and Mom's voice rang out behind us: "Well, I'm sure glad *somebody's* getting a vacation here!"

Neil didn't really play Frisbee. He lingered in the shadows between cabins, lighting stolen cigarettes that he pretended to smoke, flicking back his long hair as he ignored our games, fascinating a certain class of girl.

See the country, that's what Dad wanted. Mom would have settled for a glimpse of the inside of a spa. Me, I was after black rattlesnakes, blond tarantulas, giant desert centipedes—all creatures that, to capture Dad's phrase, really could kill you, if you gave them half a chance. I'd come equipped with The *Young Person's Guide to the Desert Southwest*, a book teeming with tongue-twisting names like *Cerapachys augustae, Centruroides sculpturatus, Crotalus cerastes*. There were full-color illustrations of deadly insects and spiders—weird animals that wore their bones on the outside, shielding their tender bits from attack. The cover displayed a scorpion, a javelina and a Gambel's quail. The name of the author—Foster R. Stevens—evoked a different age.

Printed on cottony paper, the field guide was my first book with an index, and I scribbled what passed for field notes in the blank pages at the back. Often I strayed from the subject. Sometimes I wrote about Jennifer Sung, a deer-like girl from my fifth-grade class that I'd observed with extra care before school let out.

Lizards and flies abounded in the tourist park, but more venomous fare kept strangely out of view. I sensed their presence, as though the creatures were lying low, watching us from the weeds, waiting to make their move.

Although seven years old, Willy started having relapses in the bedwetting department. It began with the first night in our new lodging, and during breakfast Dad launched into a scolding lecture about urination that made the orange juice on the table much less appealing.

"That doesn't help, you know," Mom said to him.

"What do you want me to do? Compliment the kid?"

"That's not what I mean."

"We're supposed to pretend it didn't happen?"

While they argued, Willy shrank by increments in his chair, his head sinking toward his heaving chest. Neil leaned over to offer his own input. "Swift, kiddo," he breathed. "Real swift." And while our brother stifled his sobs, Neil shot a look of complicity in my direction, to which I replied with a forced grin, feeling sorry for Willy, but not quite sorry enough that I'd stand up for him. While our parents wrangled about the best cures for bed-wetting—none of which included debating the issue in front of the offender—Neil excused himself and headed for his first shower of the day, where he'd exhaust our morning allotment of hot water.

After breakfast I found Mom kneeling down inside the front door, lifting up the tongues of our tennis shoes with a kitchen fork as she peered inside, a bludgeon of newspaper in her other hand. Someone had warned her to check our shoes each morning, in case there were bugs.

"Insects?" I pressed. "Or spiders?"

"Don't worry about it, honey." You could tell from her eyes that whatever she was looking for wouldn't have been found in a Holiday Inn.

I pulled out the field guide. Brown recluse spiders (*Loxosceles reclusa*) were to be found in the area, along with fire ants, wolf spiders and bark scorpions. None of them included tennis shoes as native habitat, but I made a decision to get up early each morning, replacing Mom's club of newspaper with the empty spaghetti sauce jar I'd fished out of the trash.

Neil spent most of the day with the headphones of his Sony Walkman clamped over his ears, tight little parentheses separating him from the rest of the family. They endowed him with the refined powers of observation and gesture usually associated with the deaf, whose ranks Mom asserted he was soon to join. That afternoon, while I studied a rock lizard outside our cabin, Neil nudged me with the toe of his Keds. He pointed toward the parking lot by the main office, where Mom and Dad stood next to a dumpster, she with her palms planted on her hips, he reaching up with a half-closed hand as if to shake the air between them, both of them speaking with animation. They were out of earshot, but we didn't need subtitles. Neil raised his eyebrows at me and clunked together the knuckles of his fists.

That night Willy kept shifting in his bed, each adjustment crinkling the garbage bag Mom had laid out beneath his sheets.

"Can't get to sleep?" I whispered across the dark.

"I wanna stay awake." There was a silence. "I don't wanna do it again."

I understood. The human body was such a puzzle. What made a person want to pee, after all? I'd felt that way once before going on stage for the school play. And then again the day I got called into the principal's office.

"Don't worry about it," I told him. "It can't happen two nights in a row. Everybody knows that."

"Really?"

"Really."

Neil called out from the bed on the other side. "You girls just about done over there? I'm trying to get some shut-eye."

Not long after, both my brothers were rasping out deep and rhythmic breaths. Only I was left awake, wondering if, after all that talk, I didn't feel a certain pressure, a tingling below my belly—and if it wouldn't be a good idea for me to trot along the hallway to the bathroom, just to be on the safe side.

The next morning I crept out to the line of shoes in the living room, spaghetti sauce jar at the ready. I lifted up the tongues and probed with the fork, but it seemed unlikely that any living creature could survive the stench of those insoles.

While waiting for others to wake, I curled up on the sofa with my book. The *Young Person's Guide* opened with a preface where Foster R. Stevens spoke plainly about the adventures awaiting young readers as they studied the hidden populations of the small. Above all, he said, don't worry about trying to check off all the species. Instead, grow familiar with the creatures you do encounter. Learn how they live and communicate. Be gentle: no matter how fierce or how timid, each animal has a right to its place on this planet. Most of all, be alert, he advised. The weapon of the weak is subtlety: the less an animal can claim to be strong, the more it aims for invisibility.

And finally, this hard idea, softened by words: All creatures eventually become food for others. It's the chain of nature. There's nothing you can or should do to stop that.

Foster R. Stevens knew how to reach me, understood me better than I did myself. Sitting on that sofa, I lingered over the pages of the preface, forming the words silently on my lips as the soothing voice of my mentor echoed in my mind.

In the empty pages at the back, I recorded my unsuccessful hunt from the morning: *Shoes, empty.* And since that didn't take so long, I tried my hand at another description, detailing the features of Jennifer Sung. In Mr. Severson's class, her straight black hair would move like a living creature each time she whirled around in her desk to glare at me with her chocolaty eyes. Best of all was Jennifer Sung's nose—a pert little accessory that worked like a weather gauge, the flare of her delicate nostrils reflecting the measure of her irritation.

* * *

Most days we went on hikes at places with strange names—Coffee-pot Rock, Boynton Vista, Courthouse Butte. They all looked pretty much the same: reddish rocks formed into Martian landscapes, sometimes rising high up in the hills, from which you could view other reddish outcroppings off in the distance. My hunt for local wildlife turned up no more than a molted snakeskin and a piece of bone, neither of which I was allowed to keep. Lizards were too numerous to interest me for long. Other animals knew how to keep their distance.

In the afternoon, back at the tourist park, the three of us would sometimes splash in the raised swimming pool. Other kids played Marco Polo, but the three of us were into dunking. Once, after Neil had stood on me under water until I came up gagging, I activated the nuclear option, sprinting across the spiky grass in my swimsuit to tell Mom and Dad, my eyes blurred by chlorine and tears, orienting myself more by sound than vision. Children's squeals called out from the pool behind. In the distance, a dog barked. From the parking lot an engine revved, slowed, then revved again. There came more voices: people chatting on a porch, and from somewhere else an angry man's voice spilled out through a screen window, answered urgently by a plaintive woman. I rubbed at my eyes with the flat of my palms, bringing the cabins into focus and finding my target. When I burst through the front door, Mom and Dad were there in the front room, standing just feet apart, like actors in a play, their scene interrupted by my surprise entrance. Mom wiped at her face and turned away, and Dad's arced arms straightened at his sides. I could still hear the revving engine and the dog outside, but the angry voices had stopped. Where had they gone?

"What do you want," Dad said. "Jesus! You're dripping water everywhere."

"Let me just...," Mom began before disappearing down the hallway. I shared a long silence with Dad until he looked away, and a moment later Mom re-emerged with a towel in hand, wrapping it around my shuddering shoulders and pulling it tight. When I looked up in shivering gratitude, I saw how red her eyes were, as though she, too, had been swimming in an overly chlorinated pool. "Let us be alone for a bit, will you?" she whispered. "Go back and play with Willy and Neil."

I'd happened upon something I wasn't meant to see, and I didn't know what to do with this special knowledge. I didn't return to the pool. Instead I strolled in the grassy area by the parking lot, prodding the dirt with a stick while the dog continued to yip in the distance.

Until that summer I'd never thought of our parents as unhappy. But all you had to do was compare us with the other families here, crowded around their identical picnic tables next to their kettle grills outside their gray cottages, barbecuing hamburgers and calling out jokes. The greasy-haired man in the cabin to our left was fat and he drank a lot of beer, but when he swatted his wife on the butt, you could tell by the way she laughed that she liked it. Mom and Dad were almost another species. I had a threadbare recollection of a scene from years earlier—when I was about Willy's age. It must have been Christmas. Mom sat on Dad's lap in a red and green plaid skirt, her arm around his neck. They wore easy, broad smiles on their faces. In the whole album of my memory, that was the one picture where you could write something like "The Happy Couple" underneath.

I didn't tell Neil and Willy about what I'd seen. Would they even care? That evening, from my bed, I watched the flypaper dangling from the fixture in the bedroom. A few representatives of *Musca domestica* eddied about the strip, and every time one of them swooped in for a good sniff, it caught fast and started to flutter. Poor things. Once their feet were mired in the glue, there was nothing for them to do but cast mournful compound glances at their buddies.

From the living room, I could hear Mom and Dad, something clenched in their voices, which the long silences didn't relax. After a while the screen door slapped closed: Dad had gone out to the porch to smoke his pipe. In our bedroom we didn't talk. Willy just crawled under his covers, grimacing as the sheet crinkled beneath him, fearing that he'd wake up in a shallow pool of urine. Neil clamped on his headphones and cranked up the volume. As for me, I turned to the preface of the field guide and lulled myself to sleep with the incantatory words of Foster R. Stevens.

The next morning, like a trapper checking his snares, I did my rounds of the shoes, spaghetti sauce jar in hand. Neil caught me and demanded an explanation. "Interesting," he said, stroking his chin. "Useful."

"How so?"

"Of course, you'll have to do it."

"Do what? Why me?"

"Because if it was *me*, Dumbo," he said, rolling his eyes, "Willy would never believe it."

"I'm not going to lie to him."

He gave me a hard stare. "Maybe you'd rather talk about Jennifer Sung's nose?"

I squinted. How on earth did Neil even know about her? I'd never once given voice to my feelings, and my thoughts had been enshrined only in the secret pages of the field guide, as private as a diary. My ears began to burn and my hands clenched into fists. But there was no way I could take him.

Neil laid out his plan, which was to start at bedtime.

That day we piled back in the car for another outing, one Mom had arranged. A woman dressed in a leather tunic rimmed with Indian beads gave us a tour of an energy vortex—a rock formation mostly notable for the number of empty beer cans it had attracted. At one point I thought I could hear the hum of secret voices, but it turned out to be a bit of *Queen* leaking from Neil's headphones. In the car afterward, Dad imitated the woman's syrupy voice, mocking her claims about magical forces. He called her a fraud. Mom didn't call her anything.

We stopped at a tourist store filled with postcards and bumper stickers, polished rocks and plastic Navajo figurines. Neil urged me to buy a rubber rattlesnake, arguing that it would make a nice surprise for Willy at bedtime. Instead, I shelled out eleven dollars for a flashlight called the ScorpioScope. *See the invisible!* it announced on the side. Tiny rays appeared around the words *black light*.

Like most impulse purchases, it was an immediate disappointment. I'd never heard of black light, and I didn't know how it worked. If a normal flashlight illuminated objects hidden in the dark, surely black light should reveal secrets by day? But it was all false advertising. The ScorpioScope did the same thing a much cheaper unit would have done, producing a soupy beam you could barely make out in daylight. On the drive to the cottage I focused it on the floor of the car, on the back of Mom's head, and even in Willy's ear. Nothing unusual appeared. It occurred to me I might not be using it right. But who needs instructions for a flashlight?

That evening, as Willy and I pulled on our pajamas, Neil nudged me hard and made a show of leaving the room. Reluctantly, I began to recite the tale. Stammering through the first lines, I warmed up, getting into the swing of it, hooting and waving my arms as I wowed Willy with a story of Arizona spirits, as powerful as Indian totems. They could travel through walls, I said, and could see your thoughts. Sometimes—and this was the important bit—they left small treasures in the shoes of good children.

"Like the tooth fairy?" Willy asked, breathless.

"That's right," I nodded. "Or the Easter Bunny."

"What kind of treasures?"

"Good luck charms. Ones that will grant any wish."

Willy turned serious. He had an ardent hope at the ready—the desire not to wake up drenched and smelling of ammonia.

They came at night, I explained, and only the first one up in the morning could find their treats.

"How come Mom didn't tell me?"

"Because this is just for kids. Grown-ups don't even know."

It was a stupid thing to say. Deep down I wanted Willy to see through it. A speck of skepticism would have kept him out of harm's way, but he was a kid born under the star of gullibility. You could cry wolf all day long, and he'd whirl around just as fast the fiftieth time as the first.

In bed that night he tossed and turned with excitement, each creak of the box spring sounding like a machine I couldn't stop. The words of Foster R. Stevens rang in my ears: Every creature has its place on this planet. Didn't that go for my little brother too?

"Philip," Willy whispered through the dark.

"What?"

"Do you think they'll come tonight?"

A word stuck in my craw, but I finally hawked it up. "Maybe."

The next morning, Willy hopped out of bed, padding barefoot into the living room while I lay clenched under the covers, waiting for the shriek. But he returned as round-shouldered as an unlucky fisherman. The next day, though, he discovered a piece of cheese in one of Dad's hiking shoes, and this struck him as a first and promising marvel. I knew better. These cubes of cheddar had come from the previous night's dinner. Neil was seeking to nudge the hand of fate. He just didn't know what bait to use.

Of all the advice from Foster R. Stevens, the lesson of patience was the hardest. We were more than halfway through our stay in Arizona, and my most interesting wildlife sightings had come in the form of the armadillos and snakes that littered the shoulders of the road—as still as stones or lengths of old hose. We did a day trip to the Grand Canyon, and while everyone else stared down, I gazed up, following the noble flight of condors—*Gymnogyps californianus*, according to the field guide.

One evening near the end of our vacation Mom placed in the center of the table a vat of macaroni and cheese with little frankfurters mixed in, the size and color of pinkie fingers. Dad greeted this dish with a minced oath, and she shot back with how, if he didn't like it, maybe we should go out for a meal. Well, maybe he *would* go to a restaurant, he allowed, if that's what it took to get a decent meal around here. Conversation lulled after that. Forks clinked against the bowls, accompanied by the sound of five jaws laboring at undercooked pasta.

Above my bed that night I made out the dark outline of the ribbon of flypaper as it twisted slowly on its string. Several black dots showed dimly, one of them still budging. I imagined myself in the fly's situation—only able to raise one foot by pushing down and sticking the other. There was no way out of glue like that. He was a goner, fully exposed on the strip of tan paper, not even able to turn invisible.

An animal crooned in the distance outside, and a flap of metal creaked in the wind. Willy wheezed in the bed to my left, and Neil's deep breaths rumbled in the dark to my right. Something was different, a hint of atmospheric disturbance, as though the barometric pressure had plummeted and a storm was brewing.

I found myself yearning for the companionship of Foster R. Stevens. The field guide lay on the night table, and all I needed to read it was a light. Although the ScorpioScope had failed in its primary task, maybe it could illuminate a page.

With the first click I understood that I'd given up on the device too soon. In the dark bedroom it didn't merely produce the standard white beam, but rather a silvery blue one with a magical hue. When I ran it across the words of Foster R. Stevens, the snowy page glowed like a living thing. I swept the shaft of light over the bed, making an edge of sheet flash bright. Socks and underwear on the floor flared. Everything white turned phosphorescent.

The back of my neck prickled. I played the light over Willy's face, his mouth gaping, his teeth gleaming. At the head of the other bed an ear stuck out from a mound of hair: Neil.

Creeping out to the living room, I approached the row of shoes by the front door. The tennies shimmered in the black light, glowing with promise. I lifted each tongue with my fingertips and peered inside the canvas grottos—as empty as always. Maybe I was too early. Maybe I was rushing it. Be patient, the guide had said.

So I settled onto the sofa and waited, playing the light across the room, struggling against the heaviness in my eyelids, jerking awake whenever the house issued a groan. I checked the shoes twice more, staggering with fatigue, still without success. Before returning to bed, wary of Willy's fate, I decided to make a stop in the bathroom, trailing a hand against the wall while guiding myself with the ScorpioScope—past our room, past Mom's and Dad's, the floor squeaking with each step.

In the dark bathroom, I dawdled on the toilet, which was always the best place to philosophize. How long would we torture Willy, I wondered. Yes, he could be a pest, but in fact it was Neil who got under my skin. And what about Mom and Dad? It was as if they'd been copying us, tormenting each other.

When a pittering noise sounded not far from my feet, I listened and waited till it came again. Snatching up the pajamas draped about my ankles, I fumbled for the ScorpioScope in the pocket, turned it on, and swooshed the narrow beam across the vinyl tiles. There, not two feet away, a creature glowed. I rubbed my eyes with the back of my fist, then focused again.

The scorpion was smaller than I expected, its body only as big as my thumb. The armor of its top was ribbed like the wrinkles of a finger. From each side, spidery legs arched out, the back ones lanky and mechanical-looking, all of them rimmed with dark hairs. Two pincers emerged from the chest, and a black dot sat in the middle of its forehead, flanked by pin-prick eyes. Then came that odd tail, crimping upward at its knuckles and curling over the back, with a hook shaped like a cat's claw sticking from the bulb at the end.

It moved forward, its legs rippling, never crossing, advancing two inches, three. Then it stopped and waited. My breath faint, I kept the light riveted on this beautiful specter. There was a wrongness to its body, to the way things bent, to the way it moved, to the strange luminescence that emanated from its insides. A sour taste rose in my throat.

It stared into the beam of light, its tail arched over its back, the pointed black tip twitching.

Scorpions don't scuttle as fast as you might think, and catching them turns out to be easy. You trap them under a plastic container, slip a piece of cardboard underneath, lift them up, and voilà. Then you deposit your prey wherever you want—for instance, in an empty spaghetti sauce jar.

And the fact was, my new friend had company. People are probably a lot happier not knowing what crawls around their home at night, especially in Arizona, but the black light made scorpions shine like little moons. They didn't care so much for the shoes by the front door after all—cheese or not—but they sure liked rooms with moisture. One skulked under the toe kick of the kitchen cabinets. I found another one (just a little guy, a scorpling) glowing in the laundry room. They seemed happy in their glass cell, the metal lid perforated by a can opener for air holes. Three scorpions, just like the three of us—Neil, Willy, and me.

I didn't share my pets. Surrendering them to Neil would have been my feudal duty, but every so often a serf gets an idea of his own. The mere thought of my spaghetti jar menagerie gave me a feeling of power, a flush of confidence.

The next day we had another excursion—a hike in a canyon outside of town. Mom and Dad had left us by the trailhead at the top of the ridge, and they'd gone hunting for the ranger office where the maps would be. I was squatting at the end of the dirt parking lot, guiding an injured termite with a stick. To the right a path led to an elevated lookout point where a bench stood next to a trash can formed of wire mesh. Willy trotted bare-chested along the rim of the shallow canyon, each step scuffing up a haze of dust.

The termite was in trouble. Somehow he'd lost two and a half legs, and he could barely inch himself forward. Soon a forager ant came roaming by and discovered this pale intruder, after which it recoiled and scurried off for help. I considered intervening, but then remembered Foster R. Stevens. *It's the chain of nature. There's nothing you can or should do to stop that.*

Soon more ants appeared. While I watched, breathless, they corralled the limping termite, blocking his attempts at escape. After parleying with their feelers, they moved in, swarming the blond monster, curling around its struggling body, applying both mandibles and stings. It didn't take long. Soon the beast lay motionless. Lapping up the juices that leaked from his pale abdomen, the ants delighted in their feeding.

A hiss came from Neil. He was leaning against the fender of the station wagon, his hands shoved into the pockets of his cutoffs, the headphones clamped over his ears. He tipped his head toward the rim of the gorge, where Willy stood several feet back from the railing, craning his neck to peer over the edge, his hands tightened into fists.

Keeping his eyes blank, Neil drew his hands from his pockets. Raising his open palms, he pantomimed a push.

My temples throbbed. Yes, a misstep could be arranged. But what about the cruelty of it? Willy was such a chicken about everything: bugs, spiders, loud noises, sudden noises, weird noises, broccoli, too many people. And heights were the worst, the pinnacle of his fear.

Neil's eyes had narrowed to slits. *Well?* his eyebrows asked. *Well?* While I delayed, he lifted his index finger and scrunched the middle of his nose. How far would I go to protect the honor of Jennifer Sung?

I rose to my feet, leaving the ants to their lonely feast.

The moan of the wind covered the sound of my footsteps as I approached my brother from behind. While Willy craned his neck to look over the edge, I raised my hands behind his naked shoulder blades, gritted my teeth, and shoved.

Down he went, palms out, knees plowing into the gravel.

A howl of terror rose up from his gut. Mom and Dad materialized, but not before I'd undergone my own metamorphosis, turning into the hero, helping a little boy to his feet, dusting him off, patting his back.

The strange thing was how Willy clung to me, as though I were a tree or a buoy—a savior.

"What happened?" Mom cried.

"He skinned his knee," I said. "But he's OK."

Willy wailed.

"Jesus Christ," Dad sputtered, his voice high. "Didn't you see how close to the edge you were? Do you want to get yourself killed?"

Mom chimed in. "Your father's right! My God. Use your head!"

Willy's body shuddered against my own while he sobbed. I told myself to be tough, but it was hard to resist the tide of guilt.

During the return to Sedona, the three of us crammed in the back of the station wagon, Willy fell asleep, exhausted from his brush with death. As his body relaxed and he slumped against me, a pearl of drool formed on his lower lip. He had a right to this place, I told myself, in this car, now, embraced by sleep. I felt an urge to stroke his blond nap of hair, but worried that Neil would see.

Then it occurred to me. So what? So what if Neil saw? What did I care? I owned three scorpions, and I could stroke Willy's hair if I wanted to.

As we rode, I wondered about Mom's strange words: *Your father's right*, she had yelled. So there still existed one thing our parents could agree on: just how stupid we kids had turned out to be.

During the next day Neil urged me to perpetrate new horrors on Willy, but I shrugged and stalled, ignoring his threats. Let him tell the world about Jennifer Sung. Being the secret master of scorpions gave me an inner strength. After all, I'd met the challenge of patience set by Foster R. Stevens—I'd lived up to his standards—and the threat of Neil's sting no longer mattered.

Eventually, he stopped insisting. Then, the next afternoon, while supposedly telling me a secret, he reached forward and shoved me in the chest, tumbling me backwards over a mass that hadn't been behind my legs a moment ago. I landed so hard that my teeth clattered, and as I picked myself up, there was Willy, rising from his hands and knees, stepping to Neil's side, a grin on his face.

I didn't care. In fact, over the previous two nights I'd added two more scorpions to my stash, each one a jewel. Foster R. Stevens would have been proud. Now five of the creatures clambered about the base of the jar. I'd dribbled a little water in, even added a beetle I found.

That poor fellow didn't last long.

The spaghetti jar was turning into a kind of piggy bank, growing heavier every day. But how do you spend a treasure like this? To what use do you put it? Imagine someone gives you a superpower, but it can be used only once. What do you do?

*　　*　　*

On the last evening we went to a restaurant. Maybe it was a peace offering by Dad. Maybe Mom had made an ultimatum. Neither of them seemed very happy about it. People at other tables enjoyed themselves, but we were like a collection of strangers seated together for convenience. Dad put away four margaritas and Mom complained about the food. Neil snapped his headphones on halfway through dinner and turned his chair away. Willy kicked at my shins.

On the drive home after dinner, I tried to ignore Willy as he jabbed me with his elbow. Up front Mom was telling Dad which way to turn, but he scoffed: he knew the route perfectly well, thank you. She insisted, and his barbed reply came back. Then, like a lost vehicle itself, their exchange veered off in some other direction, swerving into bickering I didn't understand.

Now Willy's jabs had turned into tickling. His fingers prowled over the side of my stomach, producing contortions I couldn't control. "Knock it off," I told him.

"Make me!"

I issued a second warning, but when Willy ignored it, I did try to make him, which resulted in a series of squeals.

"Mom," Neil called out without even lifting off his headphones. "Philip's hurting Willy."

But the voices from the front seat had grown louder, were drowning out our own. Willy continued to poke while I swatted his hands away. Suddenly the car was coming to a stop, so fast that I strained against the seatbelt. Dad's voice had grown loud and menacing. I realized that this was it: he was going to pull over and haul me out of the car and spank me—or worse. Maybe this was the end: the thing that would finally kill me instead of making me stronger.

"What's the matter?" Mom barked at him. "What are you doing?"

We screeched to a stop, right in a lane of traffic. Behind us a car flashed its lights.

And Dad yelled without even turning around. "You don't know what the hell you're talking about!" he said.

My mouth was dry. I had no answer. I didn't even know what he meant.

Mom's voice went shrill. "What gives you the right—?"

"Give it a rest, will you! You have no fucking idea what you're talking about."

Then I realized he was addressing *her*. They didn't even know what had been going on in the back.

The three of us shrank into the seat, hoping to be absorbed by the upholstery. We had no fucking idea what Mom had been talking about, either. We had no fucking idea about much of anything. The only fucking idea we had was to make ourselves as small as possible, to disappear.

Foster R. Stevens came to mind: Aim for invisible.

The car from behind peeled around, blasting its horn. There was a heavy silence in the station wagon—the kind where you're not quite sure if the battle is over, or if it's only a lull while the troops reload. The three of us exchanged glances in the back. After a long moment, Dad shifted into gear and the station wagon lurched forward. As we headed back to the cottage, the blacktop made the wheels hum. At every turn, the suspension creaked.

We sat on our beds while Mom and Dad shouted in their bedroom. Her voice rose and fell, sometimes angry, sometimes almost wailing. His baritone swelled and contracted, a deep rumble. We caught only snatches—a cascade of words about cooking and bugs and money and whether or not he even cared or she even tried.

"I wish they wouldn't do that," Willy whispered, giving voice to what Neil and I were too old to say. Yes, I thought: if only we could rub a magic lamp and make it all change. But how do you produce a genie like that? Where do you find that kind of power?

And yet, I did possess a genie. Five of them, in fact. Perhaps, it occurred to me, they could be used for good. We'd already seen how Mom and Dad could be united by a common enemy—the three of us. Why not these? While my brothers watched, I crouched by the bed and withdrew the spaghetti jar, exhibiting for them the churning treasures within. Willy pulled his fists toward his chest as he looked, and he issued a squeak. Neil's mouth gaped.

We implemented the plan without speaking. After they completed their admiration of my collection, we tiptoed across the shadowed hallway toward the wedge of light where their bedroom door stood ajar. While the crossfire of angry shouts continued within, I tipped it down, spilling out the living contents onto the carpet while Neil guided our troops forward with the metal lid.

Then we huddled together on my bed, the middle one, with playing cards clutched in our hands to simulate a scene of normalcy. Plausible deniability. I felt a tingle in my gut. Willy's eyes darted between Neil and me, and the little O of his mouth slowly widened into a grin. Next it was my turn. Soon even Neil was grinning, snorting. We choked the laughter back, holding our breath, waiting for the angry voices in the other room to turn to shrieks and yells. But minutes passed, and the snarling droned on and on, as if nothing had changed, as if the scorpions were just egging them along, enjoying the show, as if Mom and Dad wouldn't stop, or couldn't, no matter what the threat.

When the first shriek came, it was closer than I expected. Willy was on top of me, clawing and scrambling. Then it was Neil, his voice high like a girl's. The bed bounded with clambering bodies. When I finally I freed my face from Willy's fingers, I saw three of the scorpions moving on our floor, approaching the bed. Perhaps they had been chased this way, out-poisoned by our parent's cries. Or they had a homing instinct for the spaghetti jar. Either way, they were on the move, advancing like a platoon toward an edge of bedspread that trailed on the floor. As Neil lunged to pull the fabric up, the whole bed listed, nearly tossing us overboard.

I saw no reason to panic—until I did the math. Two of the scorpions were unaccounted for. And as the avid student of Foster R. Stevens, I knew what excellent climbers they could be.

Now three of us stood on that soft and springy mattress, the twin bed pitching right and left with our shifting weight. Willy screamed and danced, trying to keep his feet in the air. As Neil flailed to catch his balance, his hand ripped the flypaper from its string, and as the insect cemetery floated down, it unfurled over his hair and face, cementing its ribbon of corpses over his eye and cheek like a freckled mask. We hopped and jumped and screamed, clinging to each other, keeping one another from falling, waiting for Mom and Dad to burst into the room to save us.

*   *   *

Months later it would be the memory of that flypaper that endured most of all. All those evenings I had watched from my bed while the ribboned trap twisted slyly overhead, drawing new prey into its glue. No creature could ever escape on its own. But it occurred to me that if a few of them came together, they could lend each other a hand, and bit by bit they just might pull one another free, rise out of that gummy paste, and return to flight.

FOUNDERING

AFTER ALL THOSE NIGHTS of your place or mine, the first *ours* came on the overnight ferry, the one we boarded, you and I, as the storm whipped up and we pooled our dollars for a wedge of cabin in steerage, tucked deep below the waterline. Cramped in our oyster room as the vessel pitched and rocked, we joked to calm our nerves: should the vessel go down, we'd be the last to know, learning only when moisture began to weep around the edges of the sealed door. And sink we did, you recall, but only into silence, too frightened to turn off the light as the metal ceiling tipped over our heads.

Since then, like hermit crabs, we've moved from shell to borrowed shell: the upstairs duplex with squirrels in the walls and bats on the porch, followed by that ruin of an apartment in a stone building, the walls lined not with paper but actual fabric, which the kitten would claw and climb when taking a break from stalking mice; then, a leftover from the postwar, where we tiled and painted and discovered the value of our own cheap labor, where the train whistle, too close, sent the cat charging for the back door, where we quarreled and sulked and nearly parted; next was the southern tour with the mustachioed landlord, pomegranates and spiders in the garden, no heat but plenty of chilled air, and where once a roach the size of a child's hand fluttered from the vent over the bed and landed on your pregnant belly; finally, the too-square home, with space for children and a swing set, every board and pipe and fleck crying for attention, the same old cat crawling along yet a while, trees falling and growing, the tinkle of music sounding through open windows—all this while we trained to become the willing servants of teenagers.

Over time the lawn grew more vast. The years contracted. The new cats never quite belonged. Fresh paint weathered, and there were problems with the foundation. Even the children, it turned out, were only on long-term loan, and the departure of each cardboard box felt like another melon ball scooped ever closer to the rind.

And now, as this house exhales, too large and too empty, I find myself yearning for the close oyster room of the ferry. At night, we lie on the appointed sides of our broad bed just as we occupied berths during that churned crossing, silently, not admitting to our own terror for fear of spooking the other—even now, when the engine of children's voices has stalled and all has gone quiet, the vessel has tipped, and under the door we sense the first trickle of water.

RIDDLES

PEACHES.

Dead fish.

Racing dogs.

A battle on horseback.

A woman leaning over a candle in the dark.

One after another Donna trudged by these and other scenes as she made her way through the labyrinth of galleries. Clutching her handbag, she turned left, then right, then left again. Her knee ached. She walked down a long corridor, and when she entered the next chamber she swore she'd already been there.

After all, it's not everywhere you see a naked man talking to a sphinx.

Or a woman in battle armor, a wisp of a halo circling her head.

At the passage between the halls of the museum there sat a thin black man dressed in a blue uniform, so frail that an ebony cane leaned against the wall next to him. He looked up from his chair as Donna headed in his direction, her rubber soles squeaking on the marble floor with each step. She swallowed hard and applied her best smile.

"Excuse me," she said, "but do you know how I can get back to the Impressionists?"

He stared back, impassive.

"The Impressionists?" she repeated hopefully. "I'm afraid I've taken a wrong turn somewhere."

He raised his palms in a sign of helplessness, shaking his head to show he didn't understand. The radio at his belt crackled.

"Do you speak English?" she asked, and again he wagged his head. Donna didn't even have the dictionary with her—though maybe it was just as well, because then she'd have to figure out how to pronounce the words, which hadn't worked out so well at dinner last night. Or breakfast or lunch today.

So stupid, she thought as she gave up and continued down the hallway—and she wasn't referring to the guard. No, she meant herself. Really, how dumb do you have to be to get lost in a museum? There were signs, yes, but they showed the titles of galleries, named after donors or royalty or God knows what, none of which meant anything to her. It was Tom who had the map. No big deal, she'd told herself back then, twenty minutes ago. After all, there'd been the glowing green exit signs that she'd known would take her back to the main entrance, and from there she'd be able to find the right path. But instead these signs had led to ever more remote passageways and finally to a steel door with a push bar at the end of a narrow hallway. An emergency exit. Donna wasn't so desperate as to set off an alarm, but that's when she'd realized she was completely turned around.

The guidebook bragged of over six kilometers of exhibits, and although she wasn't exactly sure how great a distance that was, she knew it was long. Really long.

Where was Tom, she wondered. She'd left her husband cooling his heels in front of a painting of glowing water—a Monet (or was it Manet?)—while she popped into the powder room. Though perhaps *popped* wasn't the right word. The blue WC arrow promising toilets had in fact pointed to another blue arrow, which in turn led to another and then another. And although Donna had reached the final destination just in time for her weakened bladder, when she reemerged from the restroom, she saw that retracing her bread crumbs of signs wouldn't be easy: blue WC arrows converged on this location from multiple directions—forking paths that all looked pretty much the same.

By now Tom was probably trying to hunt her down. He'd never understood how anyone could have such a lousy sense of direction. Frankly, although she'd sometimes make a joke of it, Donna herself found it embarrassing, this inability to keep her bearings. At least when they'd landed in London, their first stop, she could blame her disorientation on the jet lag. She'd felt logy and off-balance those three days. By the time they'd boarded the Eurostar she was sleeping regular hours, but she still felt turned about—her internal compass spinning like a roulette wheel. It must be the light, she'd thought. Somehow the sun seemed to follow a different course here. Not like in Ohio.

She walked past a series of large canvases peopled with languid figures, some covered in flowing robes of pastel colors. A naked woman with a turban reclined on an oriental bed, looking over her impossibly long back, right into Donna's eyes. Other paintings teemed with crosses, arrows, thorns, pikes. A few visitors lingered before various canvases. In one gallery two slender young women chatted in a language Donna didn't understand and couldn't even identify. She hesitated at the exit from this room, taking a moment to rub her left knee. Great, she thought. A perfect time for that joint to act up. Another blue arrow pointed from the right, and Donna decided to follow it upstream. As she passed through the opening she caught a glimpse of her reflection in a glass panel, and in the instant of that glance she saw plenty. Sure enough, that was her stout figure, her double chin, her graying hair. Those were her khaki pants going by, and that was her white cotton sweater.

In short, although it wasn't the same person she'd seen in the hotel mirror this morning, it was unmistakably *her*. Donna had learned to be careful about reflections. Twenty or thirty years ago she'd been on friendly terms with mirrors, and though she'd never been uncritical of what she found in them, the quibbles had been minor. Her nose could have been a little straighter, her breasts a little rounder, her legs a touch longer. But by and large she had found herself entirely satisfactory—and so, evidently, had Tom. Three decades and as many children later it was a different story. Now she was more guarded. She had a knack for averting her eyes from the mirror when she stepped out of the bath, and she could even inspect her lipstick without allowing her gaze to drift upwards to the bags under her eyes or down toward the developing wattle of her neck. Like on TV, where they obscured a face to protect a person's identity, Donna could blur out traits she didn't want to see.

From a distance, with the right clothing and the right light, in the full-length mirror at home, and when she thought to throw her shoulders back, the results were, she thought, still respectable. It was the less choreographed encounters with herself that caused trouble. When walking in the city, a flicker would catch her eye in a store window, and before she had time to censor the image, she'd startle at the reflection of a thick, middle-aged woman meeting her gaze. Of those two selves—the one that lived in the mirror at home and the one that ambushed her on the street—which one was the real McCoy? Probably she wouldn't like the answer.

Oh crap, she thought as she entered the next gallery.

In front of her was the portrait of the woman in medieval armor, and right across from it the sphinx painting again: a young man, naked but for a cloak over his shoulder, leaning forward toward the monster as if in conversation, like he was giving directions, explaining. So odd, Donna thought. It's a woman with a lion's body and a bird's wings, and the fellow is chatting with her as if they're in a coffee shop, his left foot up on a stone.

When you got right down to it, this painting was exactly what annoyed her about all these museums. It was a large canvas, a lot of work. That much she couldn't argue with. And the painter certainly had talent—for example, the crimson fabric draped over the man's shoulder, with all those folds and the decorative hem, well, that was certainly an accomplishment, practically a photograph. And at least he'd gotten the proportions pretty much right, unlike in some of the other pictures. But what was wrong with clothing? All these naked bodies, everywhere you turned, it was *immodest*. Not to mention unrealistic. And besides, what was the big deal with all these old stories, which meant nothing to her. Why should a young man come and visit a monster? And in fact, if you looked, you could see they weren't really talking: the lion-lady just scowled at him from her cave while he leaned forward, his fingers held as if he were counting, trying to figure something out. Perhaps he was about to speak? It was hard to tell.

Maybe it had meant something hundreds of years ago, but this scene had nothing to do with Cleveland or getting children out of the house. It showed a young man ripe with ambition, one who was afraid of nothing. And you could tell just by looking at that perfect, beautiful body that he came from money. He was a man with a future, and nothing to worry about. Not like Donna and Tom, for whom this trip was their first real vacation in five years, and who were still putting their youngest through college, and who, the way things were going, would have a dickens of a time retiring. Even then they'd be stuck forever in their flat rambler on their flat yard in their flat state. No one would be painting a picture of them any time soon.

That's when she heard the English. While she stood before the sphinx painting, a couple had appeared nearby, a young dark-haired woman with deep-set eyes, dressed in a black knee-length skirt and tights, accompanied by a slim man in a tailored suit. Donna couldn't quite make out the subject of their hushed conversation, but even though the voices were accented, the words were in Donna's language.

"Excuse me," she said, and the young couple—practically kids, Donna thought—looked at her with blank stares. "Do you happen to know how to get back to the Impressionists from here?"

For a moment they stood as still as figures on a canvas, taken aback by Donna's intrusion.

"I've gotten a bit lost," she added. Then, to cushion the silence, she prattled on. "I was with my husband, you see—we've been here since lunchtime—but then I dipped into the powder room, and now I'm afraid I've misplaced him." She gave a small laugh but it sounded forced, which made her feel all the more foolish.

The girl in the skirt broke into a tight-lipped smile and spoke in lightly accented English, pointing down the corridor to the left, naming galleries, listing turns—all as casually as if giving directions in her own neighborhood. Donna hoped she could keep it straight. She felt the details already slipping away, but if she started in the right direction she stood a fighting chance of making it back. She thanked the pair energetically, and as she struck out on the indicated path, the strangers' soft conversation resumed behind her. The man said something in muffled tones. The woman laughed. And

Donna's ears burned.

As she exited the gallery she walked past an empty chair where a shiny black rod leaned against the wall, right where the frail old guard had sat. He'd stepped away, leaving his cane behind.

Her knee was hurting again. Not a sharp pain, but a dull ache that she knew would lead to fluid in the joint. She'd have to take it easy this afternoon. Assuming she made her way out of here at all, that is.

In fact, maybe she should never have made her way *in*. This was the trip she'd been asking for since, well, forever, and that Tom had been resisting. Shortly after their marriage he had promised to take her to Europe, but the time had never been right. First he needed to get settled in his job. Then she was pregnant, first with Chris, then with Shelly and Marie. And then the kids were too small. Tom had gotten his promotion. They had to save for college. Et cetera, et cetera. There was always something, always some reason to push it just a little further back, year after year.

Donna stopped at an intersection of corridors and looked in both directions. What had skirt girl said? *Right*, she thought, and she veered off past a row of small statuary.

Now, she realized, the trip had come too late. These European capitals were no place for aging women from Ohio. There exists that brief window when youth trumps money and class, when everything is possible, but if you miss it, you're too old and you no longer have an excuse for your lack of experience or worldliness. Innocence ages into ignorance. They had waited so long that she now felt out of sync everywhere they went. Earlier she had hoped to blend in with this other world. Now she was nothing but an intruder from middle age.

To make matters worse, she had to pee again.

Thinning of the muscles, her doctor had said, that was the culprit. They get weakened by childbirth, and then menopause finishes them off. Of course, Tom didn't have these bladder problems. No, in fact, he was having the time of his life here. He hadn't really cared about this trip in the first place, had said he could take it or leave it, but once they got underway, he really warmed to Europe. OK, not so much to the art museums. But he reveled in the London pubs, and in Paris it was the sidewalk cafés. She knew he enjoyed watching these slim-waisted, exotic women in the streets, and although she could hardly fault him for it—they were gorgeous, after all, even she could see that—it left her feeling bitter. This whole trip, his reaction and hers, it was the world turned upside down.

She walked past a glass panel—was it the same one as before?—and managed to ignore her reflection. A blue arrow marked "WC" pointed in one direction, and the green sign for the emergency exit suggested another. She knew enough not to fall for those traps, so she pushed on. She had a feeling she was nearly there. The entry down to the left looked familiar.

Maybe it wasn't just the muscles around her bladder. Maybe it was all of Donna that was thinning. No, not in the losing-weight sort of way. Unfortunately. More in the sense of fading. She knew she didn't turn any heads when she walked by cafés where men like Tom sat drinking their beers. They'd stopped looking at her in that way long ago. She might as well be invisible. She might as well not have come on this goddamned trip. In fact, Donna thought, she might just as well—

She halted in the passageway. In front of her stood the same naked man leaning on his spear, chatting with the same old sphinx. Across from him was the woman in armor, holding the flag. But the paintings weren't in the same place, they were backwards, as if someone had switched them around while she was out. It was insane, impossible. Then she understood: she'd gone in a giant loop, entering the same damn gallery from the other side.

Shit, Donna thought. At least she thought she had thought it, but the way a man at the other end of the room looked around, she realized she'd spoken the word out loud. Well, she didn't care. She'd had it up to here with these stupid hallways by now. All she had to do was walk up and put her finger on the sphinx's nose and every alarm in the museum would go off. She knew it. Guards would come running. That sure as hell would get her out of here.

Yet she didn't touch a thing. Instead, she took a deep breath and clenched her grip on her purse. Something about the sphinx painting annoyed her, wouldn't let her go. That young man with his foot on the stone, he exuded such confidence. Yes, he was talking to a monster with a lion's claws and the wings of an eagle, but you could bet he'd come out all right. He had his whole life in front of him. Probably he'd start a family. The velvety cloak draped over his shoulder told you he was used to luxury. Everything would be easy.

Hah, she thought. Give him twenty or thirty years and then see how he likes it.

All right. Enough was enough. She'd follow the signs back to the bathroom, have a pee, and then ask directions in every damn room until she got out of this place. Tom could find her back at the hotel. In fact, as far as she knew, he was already there. That is, if he wasn't out at some café drinking his beer and ogling the locals.

Then, as she turned away, something caught her eye and she glanced back one last time, doing a double-take as if startled by her own reflection, twisting mid-step and pinching something delicate in her knee. At the bottom of that painting, sticking up from the rubble below the sphinx, was, of all things, a human foot. And not just that: the ball-shaped thing next to it, which looked a bit like another stone, it was a skull. Nearby there lay a line of ribs. Good grief. Those were *human bones* piled up beneath the perch of the she-monster. Donna felt the vague recollection of a story.

She stepped back, and her bad knee nearly buckled.

What was the big idea? Why would an artist stick a bunch of bones into the corner of a fancy-pants picture? Clearly that was what happened to people who came to talk to the monster, and yet the naked young man wasn't bothered. Did he even understand what was at stake? He seemed confident, untouchable—as if he had all the answers.

And then, though she didn't know where it came from, Donna felt a surge of anger welling up inside. No, not anger: *indignation*. How dare they, she thought. She hadn't come five thousand miles to see *this*.

She hobbled toward the doorway. The guard's black cane still rested against the wall, and since no one was looking, she borrowed it, leaning on this third leg as she made her way to the brown leather bench in the middle of the gallery, plopping herself down. My God, but she was tired!

How *dare* they? She thought again. Here she was, stuck in the middle of this goddamned maze, her knee hurting like the dickens, with Tom off doing God knows what God knows where, while she just turned in circles, growing hungry and thirsty, trapped in a place made for young, pretty people—sophisticated types who didn't need signs that a normal person could understand, and where even the paintings were calculated to taunt her, to remind her, to trick her into seeing things she didn't want to see. To think that she had begged for this trip! What in God's name had she been thinking? What was the point? And what on earth were you to do after the scales have tipped in your life, after the children have gone, and all you have left to do is wait?

Donna didn't know the answers to these questions. She focused on her anger, on Tom, on the purse clutched in her lap, on the painting. A flurry of images flashed through her mind: planes, hotels, housekeeping, girls, shops, beer, the babel of tongues. As quickly as she flicked through these thoughts, their edges darkened, like water wicking into a paper towel. Her lip quivered.

That handsome young man, calmly laying out replies to the sphinx in front of him—Donna didn't buy it. It was a lie, this picture, like all the rest of the paintings. A whole museum of lies. There were no answers. It was a waste of time to look. The only thing was to keep moving forward.

She felt drained. Her knee ached. And to top it all, she felt that pressure down below, where the muscles had thinned. She closed her eyes and shook her head. There was no use fighting it. And because there was nothing else to do, she sucked in her breath and struggled to her feet, wincing as the knee took her weight. She didn't allow her eyes to wander as she limped out of the gallery. A blue arrow pointed to the right, and Donna followed it.

THE
PHRASEBOOK

IN THE END we didn't even speak the same language. It was like reading from a traveler's phrasebook, all the entries approximate, supplemented by pantomime. Even if we managed to pronounce the questions, the answers came back unintelligible.

Do you speak English? But no, neither of us did. Not anymore. That tired old language had collapsed, replaced by two separate dialects. They drew on familiar sounds but skewed them with different meanings, bending them to new and impenetrable grammars. We tried speaking louder, to no avail.

I am lost. Can you help me? Our paths had crossed and diverged, re-crossed and re-diverged. There'd been twists and curves. Even though we lived together, ate together, slept together, we lost sight of each other for long stretches, passing by without seeing, making love without speaking, and then bumping into each other in the kitchen, surprised to find that since our last meeting we'd each grown a little more foreign.

Where does this train go? We hadn't even known we were moving. Who knew there was a destination? That's what happens: you wake up to find yourself a homesick tourist, but you've lost your return ticket. You can't locate your passport. Probably there are agencies that could help, but to go where? You thought you were already home.

One. Two. This much you understand, fingers serving as an aid. But what do the numbers mean? Is it a sum, or parts? A couple, or individuals? An addition, or a separation? Could it be an order, a sequence? If so, what is the next step? And as you flip through the pages you discover that, as in most phrasebooks, no one bothered to include *zero*.

It hurts here. And you gesture everywhere, showing the multiple points of impact.

Something went wrong. The turns were too sharp. We were going too fast. We thought it was all under control. By the time we understood, it was too late. The collision was too violent. The damage had been done. Only the formalities remained, the paperwork.

Please, I need to report an accident.

THE
SPIRIT
OF THE
DOG

CALEB WAS A BLUSHER. Always had been. As a kid, they called him a mommy's boy just to watch him flush crimson. He'd counted on puberty to help him hide his cheeks, but in high school his beard came in wispy and blond. At the public library he had read about breathing techniques and mind games, to no avail. His body refused to lie. Always it bore witness against him, which was exactly what worried him now as barrel-chested Ross worked his way down the line of men, interrogating them one at a time, the braided leather bullwhip coiled in his hand.

Caleb tried arching his eyebrows and sinking his chin, relaxing his jaw. He decided he could take a stand if his cheeks sold him out. Only twenty years old, he was unpracticed at physical combat. But there were times a person might surprise himself.

He felt a stirring deep inside, as if an unused muscle were coming to life.

Ross was talking to Art now, leaning in as he fingered the bullwhip. That cowhide strap was practically an extension of the foreman's arm, of his will. Caleb had seen how Ross could split an apple at fifteen paces, or pick off a snake, if one was handy. It was a useful prop, good at snagging people's attention.

While waiting his turn, Caleb squinted into the sun as it melted into the ridge. A few hundred yards away, the dirt path began its sloping descent into the darkening bowl of the uranium mine, a spiraling peel of road leading down to the pan—a broad, flat surface that two years ago had still been hidden under a mountaintop.

Now Ross stood before silver-haired Tennessee, scrutinizing this lanky, respected member of the crew, who returned the boss's stare with a look halfway between amusement and affront. Not a hint of red.

From behind came a sizzle of whispers from the Mexicans. Who could blame them? It was Diego's wallet that had gone missing that day, with all the pictures of his kids back in Juárez. The poor guy had danced around the locker area, patting at his pockets, searching under the benches, crying out for help. The detail that threw everyone was the fifty-three dollars in bills littering the floor.

And the wallet wasn't the only item to have gone missing over the past two weeks.

From the chatter, Caleb made out *espíritu* and *perro*, the words sticking his conscience like a pin under a fingernail. They were talking about Patch, as if that amiable hound had padded back from the grave to plunder their lockers or steal personal effects from the glove boxes of their pickups. An act of revenge.

Ross lumbered over. "Oh, for crying out loud, Diego," he said. "It ain't no goddamn spirit of no fuckin' dog."

Diego stepped forward. The chatter went quiet. "You don't know that, Ross."

The foreman glared. It was rare for a man to speak back. "What the fuck you think this is, Diego—a summer camp? Are we telling *ghost stories* now? Is that what we're doing?"

And because Caleb was at hand, was the youngest and arguably the most malleable, Ross turned to him for confirmation, leaning in close enough to share the acrid smell of his breath. "What do you think, Caleb?" he pressed. "Are we dealing with ghosts here?" His voice floated the words like an honest question—while his eyes prompted the answer.

The temperature rose in Caleb's smooth cheeks. He knew what the foreman expected. By their nature miners were solitary hunters, like coyotes, and it took a blend of guile and menace to keep them operating as a pack.

"No sir. I've never seen a ghost," he replied to Ross's visible satisfaction. That much was true. No, the only haunted place was Caleb's memory, where the phantom of Patch tugged at sticks and fetched rocks. Then that new muscle deep within him flexed. It would cost him, but he decided to speak. "That said," he added, "I've never seen radioactivity either, though I reckon this mountain's ripe with it."

Ross's expression contracted into sourness. The chaw of tobacco traveled from one cheek to the other, and he twitched to the right, sending a dart of caramel-colored spittle into the dirt. The Mexicans whispered again, more urgently. Then Tennessee piped up. If it was the supernatural we were dealing with, he said, maybe we'd better start with a round of stiff drinks. Art emitted a gravelly chuckle, and Curt drawled out a string of profanity.

The whistle blew, announcing the end of the day, and the group broke formation, everyone heading for the lockers in the machine shed.

"Y'all know whose fault this is," Ross called out behind them. He brandished his coil of bullwhip toward the white mobile home that served as the geology laboratory. "It's *her*," he said. "Y'all know it."

But that was just it: they didn't know. For now, they filed into the locker area and retrieved their gear for the night. Five minutes later the caravan of pickups and four-by-fours started down the mountainside. Caleb rode with Art, not talking, letting his head jostle against the frame of the door as the other man eased the vehicle over the bumps of the graded road. In the rearview mirror the geology lab began to recede from view. Penny Nolan still hadn't emerged.

Who could blame her, after what had happened? She'd done her best to tame imaginations—donning those steel-toed Red Wings, the canvas cargo pants, the rugged khaki shirts. And she knew the script of authority. But thirty-two rough men worked that open pit, forty miles away from the nearest town and hundreds more from their wives and girlfriends. When the mine's new geologist had climbed out of her pickup truck six weeks earlier, a slender woman, just thirty years old, with flaming red hair and a galaxy of freckles— a black and white and brown mutt bounding out after her—Caleb had smelled the perfume of trouble.

What the fuck did Avalon Mining think they were doing, Ross had groused, putting a piece of meat like *that* in front of them? It didn't help that she demanded a slew of immediate changes, even telling Ross, right in front of everyone, how the blast patterns had to be redone. If only she'd known, Caleb thought, how the foreman's eyes had narrowed when she turned away, and how Ross had wheeled about to see the men dropping their gaze to their feet. The next day he'd barked out commands, humiliated men with criticism, and singled three of them out for discipline—all of which met with shrugs and murmurs. It was as if the pail of Ross's authority had sprung a leak, and no matter how hard he worked, he couldn't fill it back up. Not until he found a way to mend it.

The next day, when Penny asked Ross in front of the others to stop by the geology trailer, he sang out a *Yes ma'am*, with exaggerated deference, waiting until she was out of range before suggesting what he'd do her when he got there. Laugher erupted among the men, and Caleb blushed. With a single stroke Ross had put himself back in the lead.

So now, was it any surprise that he would accuse Penny of being involved in the thefts, when he was losing his hold over them again?

In one sense, Caleb figured the Mexicans were right: the recent incidents did have to do with the dog. But everyone knew that Ross was wrong: Penny Nolan had no hand in it. The day Art lost his ancient Dodgers cap, she wasn't even on the premises. When the side mirror disappeared from Curt's new F150, leaving an amputated stump of wires, she'd been collecting samples in the pit. And the afternoon Caleb's blue and yellow letter jacket vanished—the leather one his mother had given him just months before she died—Penny Nolan was nowhere to be seen.

*   *   *

She'd given Caleb the jacket during his senior year. Her plan had been to hang on until his high school graduation, but the cancer decided otherwise. Before it took her, she'd made Caleb promise to go to college. He did try it. But after the first term he'd packed up his things. What was the point?

That was when he found work with Avalon Mining. He started as a gofer, running errands and fetching equipment. But after Dale got fired for drinking on the job, half of Caleb's time went to operating the drill rig. He'd bore a grid of four-inch-wide holes twenty feet deep, then tie lengths of detonation cord to turd-like tubes of gel-ignite. These he would lower all the way down, packing the cavities with ANFO pellets. Next he'd knot the pigtails together with more cord. Every two or three days, while the crew sat on benches eating their lunch, it was Ross who'd drive down into the pit, stick a blasting cap on the cord, and connect the wires. When he got back up to the machine shed he'd push the button, and between mouthfuls of ham sandwich the men would watch the earth rise in a puff, levitate for an instant, and then collapse. A man-made thunder crack would sound, and then it would rain gravel, sometimes as far as the shed.

Like riders on the backs of great beasts, Art and Curt and Tennessee would steer the D10 dozers into the pan and bite through crusts of rock with steel tusks, breaking them into gobbets for the scrapers, mechanical jaws that slid along the ground and swallowed whole landscapes of rubble into their low-slung gullets. The Mexicans trailed behind on foot, probing with Geiger counters, planting orange flags to map where the deposits were rich.

Layer after layer they went, always deeper, uncovering more and more, bringing hot ore to the surface. They revealed the earth's secrets despite herself, as if shaming her.

Because he could drill blast holes faster than the crews could clear the debris, Caleb still had time for errands, fetching reels of det cord for himself, grabbing toolboxes for others, sometimes toting ore samples up to Penny Nolan in the trailer. That first time, her dog had wrinkled his black snout at Caleb's approach, emitting a cautionary growl.

"Don't mind Patch!" Penny said. "He's a sweetheart pretending to be a brute." And she ruffled the fur behind his ears.

Caleb didn't rush. With Penny's encouragement Patch soon understood the boy was welcome. The dog became Caleb's friend, gamboling over whenever he arrived, nuzzling his hand, his tail whipping back and forth.

When not at Penny's side, Patch ran free around the trailer and the machine shed, sniffing, chasing pocket gophers. He knew how to sit and beg and roll over and even smile a kind of bare-toothed smile—and Caleb would reward him by scrubbing his white belly with his knuckles, or offering him bits of sandwich.

With the dog as his excuse, Caleb dawdled during stops at the trailer. Sometimes he chatted with Penny, but he liked to sit in her presence even if she was too busy to talk. She taught him how to grind stone into grit for the assays, how to run the spectrometer, how to record the results in the log. Ten years older than he was—the age of his English teacher in high school—she played the advisor, asking about his past, his future, urging him to go back to school. Once, when they were playing fetch with the dog, Penny caught Caleb watching her. He blushed and looked away.

There's no shame in not being able to lie, his mom used to say. But still, he sometimes wished he could conceal his feelings.

No one else stopped in at the trailer. The men muttered about Penny. Having a woman at the mine wasn't natural, they said. It changed things. Sure, they got to eye her ass every time she walked by, but in return they were supposed to watch their mouths. That didn't stop the comments and jokes that flew behind her back, the occasional wolf whistle. They undressed the redheaded geologist with their words, describing acts Caleb didn't want hear about, sometimes within earshot of her trailer.

He was pretty sure she knew how the men felt about her presence. But she hadn't understood the scale of the problem, as if she'd been looking at it through the wrong end of a pair of binoculars.

And because they couldn't do anything about Penny, the men turned against Patch. It had nothing to do with dogs in general. To the contrary. It was the specific resentment of this particular animal, which somehow outranked them and remained loyal to a mistress they couldn't abide. Curt took to kicking Patch in the hindquarters when Penny was away. One day Ross pulled his bullwhip off the nail in the shed and put on a terrible spectacle, making the dog yelp with electric snaps of leather. One of the men brought up the idea of a poisoned steak. One by one they took to taunting Patch, or at best ignoring him, even men who had dogs of their own.

Caleb now realized that this was when he should have stepped in. But how could he stand up against the same group he was trying to join? Mixing with these older, coarser men had been like a mountain climb, ripe with false steps and loose handholds. Back in town, over beers, they woud bait him, goading him about girls. Most of the other guys paid for women. Art and Curt had families off in Cheyenne and Provo, but that didn't stop them. *Little boy,* they called Caleb, jabbing him in a half-friendly way. *Time to grow up,* they said. *Time to learn how to ride.*

And he'd feel the red flood across his face.

He wished he could say he hadn't had a choice, but that would have been a lie. He did try it once, for forty dollars, with a skinny, brown-haired girl, about his age. He thought they'd maybe been in high school together, though he didn't know her name. He hadn't been able to finish, and the girl had just stroked the back of his head, his face buried in the pillow.

The day Patch disappeared, they'd been sitting with their lunches by the machine shed while Ross prepared for a detonation. Penny hadn't left her trailer, but the dog was out, lying in the shade and watching the men eat, panting from the heat. The foreman had bundled up his kit and was halfway to his truck when he halted, turned, and eyed the dog. He stood long enough for people to notice, long enough for conversations to trail into silence. Then he clicked his tongue and approached, holding his hand out in a friendly fashion. But the dog had learned to be wary of the bullwhip man with the hardhat, and he backed away, his tail sinking between his legs.

Which is when Ross had turned to Caleb. "Hey, lover-boy. Grab the mutt for me."

At first Caleb hadn't understood, or hadn't wanted to. He looked around at Curt, Art, Zero, Tennessee—whose eyes were now all on him. Was he in the group or not?

"I don't think he'll come," Caleb began, but Ross crossed his arms over his broad chest and waited. Caleb approached with an outstretched palm, and as Patch sniffed and wagged, he looped a finger under his collar.

"Hang on," Ross grunted, and he returned from the machine shed with a length of rope. Caleb felt a rise of nausea. The foreman dragged the whimpering dog to the truck and slammed him in the cab. As the pickup rumbled toward the bowl of earth, Patch peered out the back window, his ears nearly flat against his head.

Twenty minutes later, when the pickup reappeared, Ross was alone.

"Where's Patch?" Caleb said, but the foreman just ran his tongue along the inside of his fleshy lips. He opened the detonator kit on the hood of the truck.

"Ross," Caleb started again, swallowing down a metallic taste. "What did you—"

The foreman stopped him with a stare. "Never you mind," he said.

Then Caleb watched him press the red button with his thumb. The earth shuddered underfoot and soon a cloud rose from the open basin. A moment later came the pitter-patter of falling gravel.

And Caleb felt something tear inside of him.

That afternoon Penny searched for her dog, clapping and calling, her voice going shrill, as though a gangrene of worry were spreading inside her. She spoke of snakes and checked out the steep edges of the gorge. At the end of the day, as the guys packed their gear, she grabbed men by the sleeve, pleading for information, begging for help.

They shook their heads, avoided her eyes. When she came to him, Caleb stared at his boots, his eyes flickering as if he were blinking away grit.

"Caleb?" she said. "Caleb?"

Since childhood he had thought there were just two kinds of blushing: one for what you wanted to do but didn't dare, and another for what you'd done and shouldn't have. But it turned out there was a third kind, reserved for what you should have done but didn't—and this one was the worst of all.

That was how Penny learned—just by looking at Caleb. She didn't know the specifics, but the specifics didn't matter. She staggered back from him, speechless.

In the dark of his closed eyes it wasn't Penny that Caleb imagined, or even Patch. It was his mother, as she'd looked during that final year, her face lined with compassion, now tinted with disappointment. It was more than he could bear.

* * *

The next items to disappear were both precious and trivial: a silver Saint-Christopher medal from Jaime's dashboard, Ole's rabbit-foot keychain (but not the keys), and Tennessee's Blackwell pipe—the one he'd had for years.

"Judas Priest," Tennessee cursed, losing his cool for once. "I've had just about enough of this!"

One object a day. It felt both sinister and inexorable. They wondered what would be next. "It's because of the dog," men were saying, and not just the Mexicans now. People were agitated. It might start with tobacco pipes and letter jackets, but who knew where it would end? They'd all heard stories about workplace disasters, injuries and even deaths. But this steady nibbling away, this creep of anxiety? It was unknown territory.

Ross instituted searches. He and Joel patted the men down at the end of every day. They performed spot checks on lockers and car trunks and lunch buckets. Ross made a show of combing through every corner of the laboratory, and Penny Nolan herself had to empty her pockets.

But even when Art's Mossberg hunting rifle disappeared from his truck rack—a big, heavy thing—they turned up no clues.

The men were looking to Ross, as foreman, to handle it. But despite his girth, all he had now was the smallness of words. "When I find the fuckhead that's doing this," he announced, "we're settling it here." He nodded toward the loops of bullwhip over his desk. "No police. Just the two of us."

Behind his back men grumbled. They wanted action, not threats. And it galled them to become the object of suspicion when they were already the victims.

Talk turned to Penny. They were waiting for the day she'd up and leave, as if that might lift the curse. But mining attracts hard people, people with the will to break through stone. Caleb knew she was as headstrong as the rest.

* * *

Every so often Caleb would finish a grid of blast holes, and over lunch Ross would drive down to sound the air horn and set the fuse. The earth would rise and fall, a thunderhead of dust would billow. The clearing of rubble would continue, and Caleb would start afresh.

But objects continued to disappear. After ten days, the Mexicans quit. It was a late afternoon and Caleb watched Diego talking with Ross by the shed, the smaller man shaking his head in refusal as the foreman's voice grew louder. Everyone was watching. In an hour Diego and his crew had cleared out all their gear and driven away.

Ross was white with a cold fury. He stalked over to the geology trailer and pounded on the door. When he disappeared inside, the men listened to the muffled yells, followed by Penny's shrill replies.

Tennessee pointed out that nothing had been taken from Penny Nolan herself, which led to speculation again about the spirit of the dog, back to protect his mistress.

Ross selected Caleb to serve as a guard at night, sacking out in the machine shed. The very first evening, after the caravan of pickups and four-by-fours snaked down the mountain, Penny Nolan emerged from her trailer, toting a knapsack in one hand, her shoulders bowed. She bristled when she spotted him standing there in the weary light—a lone man meeting a lone woman on a mountainside.

He didn't know how people managed to communicate with their eyes, to say complicated things with such awkward tools. He tried, but maybe it was too dark. Or maybe, he figured, Penny wasn't in the mood to read.

She walked past him as if he weren't there.

"Dr. Nolan," he said, and when she didn't stop, he called out again, a touch louder. "Penny."

Now, at the door of her pickup, she paused, her back to him.

"I just wanted to say," he began. But then he wasn't sure. What did he want to say? How it all happened? How the guys had felt hemmed in by her presence? How Ross balked at taking orders from a woman? How the way she ignored the lewd comments and leers had only made it worse? How they'd taken it out on an innocent dog, a sort of sacrifice that Caleb still didn't understand?

Or maybe he should tell what finally happened. How they'd all been a part of it. How no one was without guilt. Especially Caleb who'd seen it coming, had been drawn in, and had failed to stop it.

Penny opened the door to the pickup and climbed in.

In lieu of speaking, Caleb blushed.

*　*　*

It was a long night alone at the machine shed, and in the chill air he missed the warmth of his letter jacket. He thought about his mother. After the moon went down, the Milky Way deepened, a swoosh of speckles sprayed onto the sky. Half a mile away lay the lip of the gorge, and from the far side came the rise of a growl, the sound of a mountain lion at the edge of its territory. An answer came from closer by, and for a while these two cats, maybe potential mates, called across the abyss, unable to cross.

He studied the sky, examined the dark hulk of the machine shed, peered down into the black maw of the pit. Telling people what you felt was like mining, he thought. Everything of value was buried under a mantle of stone, and to bring it to the surface you needed hard work and sometimes high explosives. He was drilling his grid of holes, but it was a damned hard shell of rock.

He stayed out there every night, though he never had anything to report. Nothing disappeared during the hours of darkness. But every single day another object would vanish—even though people hardly brought anything with them any more. Once it was Neil's lunch box—not the food, which was left behind on the wooden bench, but the metal box itself, which he'd owned for a long time. Then Zero's white sneakers went, the old ones he pulled on after work, for comfortable driving. Next was the fly-fishing rod Beadle kept locked in the long tube that mounted to his roof-rack—the whole tube had vanished.

During daylight hours Caleb worked the drill rig and ran errands in the pickup. He took ore samples up to Penny's trailer, knocking softly and leaving them outside her door. At night he thawed dinners in the microwave of the machine shed. Sometimes he made a campfire. Once he found a snake in his sleeping bag. But he was growing accustomed to the noises of the mountain—whose very breath he could hear once the equipment fell silent.

Then, one afternoon, while Caleb drilled in the pit, the air horn sounded. One after another the machines powered down, and up on the rim stood Ross in miniature, a barrel on spindly legs, the arms waving, a voice hawking. The men climbed off the dozers and rigs, slowly piling into the available pickups and starting the climb to the shed. Ross was there waiting, glowering, his arms folded. He spat a streak of tobacco into the dirt.

He had even bullied Penny out of her trailer, lining her up with the others in the hangar area of the shed while he strutted before them. His face was veined with purple, and one eye looked larger than the other. He'd had enough of this *fucking around*, he said, carving the words with the blade of his tongue. He was going to *kill the motherfucker* who'd done it. But still the men didn't understand—not until he jabbed a finger at the empty space where the bullwhip used to be.

"Which one of you took it?" His voice whistled.

The question met with an uneasy silence. Caleb heard the shuffling of feet. A June bug made ticking noises as it charged against the overhead light, and a metal flap creaked with the breeze outside. Everything felt slow and clear.

Caleb's face seared. He knew he'd be glowing like a beacon, but he didn't bother raising his eyebrows or slackening his jaw. He was done imitating innocence.

Ross had started at the far end of the line, where Penny Nolan stood erect, her red hair cascading over her shoulders, her chin high. He towered over her, pressing in with his great belly. "I know you're part of this," he breathed into her face. "Don't think you're getting away with it just because of your fucking dog."

The accusation left a vacuum, a hollow that begged to be filled. But Penny Nolan held her tongue, reducing her eyes to slits, looking Ross up and down, and shaking her head almost imperceptibly, the way one assesses something vile or foul. It was an expression unmarred by fear, Caleb noted. Not even hatred. Her eyes held an ingredient he couldn't name, a look designed to make things wither. She didn't back away—no, she wouldn't let Ross have that—but after the silence ripened she slipped to the side and stepped without hurry toward the door.

"We're not done!" Ross said to her back.

Penny paused, then rolled her thin-eyed gaze over Ross again, looking right through him. He took a step forward, but she halted him with a snort. His fists trembled. Caleb could see he was trying to muster up a threat, but it was no use. He was no longer the foreman. He'd shrunk into nothing more than a fat, angry man.

Now Penny began to scrutinize each of the men, one after the other. One by one they turned their heads, their shoulders rounding, their chins sinking toward their chests.

Caleb forced himself to meet her gaze. Penny had reserved for him her most corrosive look of all, her eyes less angry than sad, halfway between disappointment and betrayal. He kept his eyes fixed on hers, subjecting himself to her scrutiny, trying to lay himself bare. And when Penny finished her examination, her brow had wrinkled. Her lips opened with a question she didn't ask. Caleb felt not quite redeemed or purified, but at least somehow understood.

Then she was gone, the door swinging closed like the seal of a vault.

Still the June bug battled with the lights overhead.

Tennessee coughed. "You know, fellows," he said, "I believe I'll be moving along. Time to look for new opportunities." He stepped forward and tipped his hat to Ross, who couldn't protest, not against Tennessee, not in front of everyone.

Next it was Curt, then Art, then Zero. Then there was no keeping track.

They peeled off one after the other. Soon everyone had quit. Folks were clearing out lockers, packing it up, piling gear into trucks. Ross stormed and gestured, yelling first, arguing next, soon almost wheedling, promising to lighten up. But the cars and pickups were loaded, and soon the caravan began to curl its way down the dirt road in the twilight.

From the machine shed Caleb watched Ross's pickup trailing

behind the others. Probably the foreman hoped to bribe them in town with a few rounds of drinks. But Caleb suspected the men were beyond the reach of alcohol.

He, too, would be moving along, as soon as he collected his things—the sleeping bag, his backpack of clothes. He'd trek down to the highway, and from there hitch a ride. The direction didn't matter. Still, he was sorry to be leaving this mountainside where big cats called through the night and the campfires warmed him. And he had no clear destination. Maybe he'd go back to school. Maybe not.

When he exited into the deepening dusk, Penny Nolan's truck still stood outside. The trailer door creaked open, spilling light, and out she came, lugging a box of files. Caleb dropped his head and started toward the road.

"Caleb," she called.

He marched on.

"Caleb," she said again.

But what was the use of talking? He stared at the ground between his feet while she approached.

"It was you, wasn't it?"

His face warmed. It was then he realized that there existed even a fourth kind of blushing, one divorced from shame, somehow more akin to pride.

She touched his sleeve. "How'd you do it?"

He told her everything. What Ross had done. The role he'd played. How bad he'd felt. And the decision he'd made. At first there'd been no real plan. Just a desire. A wish to make others feel a tiny bit of what she'd experienced. A kind of loss. It had to be visible and involuntary. It had to touch them.

He had the access—all those errands for blasting supplies, some of them not strictly necessary. He knew everybody, what they owned and what they liked. And he had a place to put things: a grid of twenty-foot deep holes that grew larger every day, that he filled with explosives, and that every now and then Ross himself would detonate, obliterating any evidence.

He hadn't done it for revenge. No, it wasn't quite that. Instead, he thought of it as a lesson in shame.

"And your letter jacket?" she said.

He shrugged. He was as guilty as the others. He'd needed to make a sacrifice, too. Besides, if he hadn't, they'd have known who it was.

They stood together in the dark for a long while.

"So," she said. "Would you like a ride?"

That voice, somehow it lifted him up. It helped him breathe again.

"Yes, Ma'am," he said. "I would. I'd very much like a ride."

He threw his gear in the bed of the truck and climbed up on the passenger seat next to Penny Nolan—the seat formerly occupied by the brown and black figure of Patch.

SINCERELY
YOURS

THE LETTER ARRIVED in a plain brown envelope, my address showing through its plastic window. No return information. The postmark was illegible. Junk, I figured, but just to be sure I grabbed a butter knife off the kitchen table and slit it open. Out slipped a single sheet of paper which, when unfolded, revealed the logo of our gas and electric utility, followed by a few lines of print. To be more precise, it was the logo of the multinational that had recently acquired the holding company that had earlier merged with our gas and electric utility. Frankly, it's been hard to keep it all straight.

This is what I read:

E***, Inc.
P.O. Box 28271
Bethesda, MO 42002

Dear Mrs. <Name>,

It has come to our attention that payment for your last billing is overdue. You have a current balance of: -$52.17. We assume the lateness of your payment is oversight, and we request you send a check or credit card information no later than <DATE1>, after which we will need to refer your account to collections.

If you wish to dispute this billing, please respond to the address above, or contact your service agent at the number below.

Yours sincerely,

Natasha Naranski
Customer Service Representative
721-9394

That was it—it really did show <NAME>, right after they mis-identified my gender. Now, I'm not what you would call an alpha male, a top dog, a shining example of the species, but still, that last bit seemed a little uncalled for. And the date truly was shown as <DATE1>. I thought: Really? DATE1 *already*? Golly but time flies. And Natasha had actually written the words "the lateness of your payment is oversight"—without an "an." Was it a typo, or had E*** outsourced all its customer service to Kiev, where women named Mika and Natasha and Tatiana assembled English sentences like jigsaw puzzles? Even the return address seemed weird. Bethesda, *Missouri*? Shows what I know.

But the basic complaint about non-payment did not especially surprise me. This is the kind of stuff that happens every time big companies gobble each other up. You send in a check and it circles the globe two or three times before it lands in an account. You pay so many bills and write so many checks that it's hard to keep track of them—and to tell the truth, who wants to? In fact, who knows? Maybe I did screw up. The next day I had a chance to look into it, and after going through my check register and making a few calls, I put pen to paper. Call me old-fashioned, but I still like to write out personal notes longhand.

Dear Natasha,

Thank you for your recent message, which I received two days ago. I write you now to let you know that there appears to be an error. I don't mean to accuse *you*, of course, or anyone at E***. Far be it from me to throw the first stone. Personally, I goof up all the time. But my bank has informed me that check number 3042, in the amount of $52.17, cleared quite some time ago, which means, I think, that my good name is also in the clear. What a relief for both of us! To assist you in putting the record straight, I have attached a photostatic copy of the check in question.

Actually, I tried to call you up to share this good news, but the number you supplied in your epistle does not appear to be local. Or rather, it *is* a local number, but locally it belongs to a Mrs. Hazel Whitten, whom I believe to be rather elderly. I took the liberty of dropping E***'s name during a pause in her yelling. She became rather exercised when I began to speak about money. Should she happen to call you, I'd appreciate it if you could reassure her of my good intentions.

Anyway, all this to say that I don't have your area code. (On that same score, I cannot locate Bethesda, Missouri in my atlas, which, though not a recent printing, seems to include most US cities. I hope this letter reaches you.)

If any further action is required on my part, please let me know.

Oh, and for the record, the last time I checked I was still a Mr., so you might want to update your database.

Yours, etc.

That was that. I pictured myself standing in front of a giant *Mission Accomplished* banner. I had crushed this one. The evidence was irrefutable. So I resumed my life: going to work, washing my clothes, playing with the cat. It's a pretty simple existence, really.

Then, about ten days later, it turned complicated again. I came home one evening and pulled out the mail, and what did I find but another one of those coarse, brown envelopes—a clone of the first one: same first class stamp, same faint postmark, and even the same smudges on the flap. They must print these things by the thousands, and the smudge marks come from the rollers on the machinery. I can't say I wasn't curious, so I ripped it open. In my hands was another letter from my friend Natasha:

E***, Ltd.
P.O. Box 28271
Bethesda, MO 42002
SECOND NOTICE

Dear Mr. <Name>,

In our letter of <DATE1> we brought to your attention an overdue bill in amount of: $52.17. We still await payment on this account, and it is with regret that we must now add interest (21% APR) and a late penalty of $25.00. Please send your payment in the amount of: $78.12 no later than <DATE2>, or we will be forced to refer your account to collections.

If you wish to dispute this billing, please respond to the address above, or contact your service agent at the number below.

Yours sincerely,

Natasha Naranski
Customer Service Representative
721-9394

Well, at this point Natasha was beginning to rub me the wrong way. It's like she hadn't even read my letter. Or *had* she? After all, somehow my manhood had been restored: I was back to my rightful place as Mister Name. But she made no mention of the copy of the check I had sent. Otherwise it read like the same impersonal gibberish. Natasha was still having trouble with her dates (she needs to get out more, I told myself). And there was that phrase: "overdue bill in amount of." I mean, whatever happened to the "the"? Why is it that Natasha kept dispensing with articles, those unthanked workhorses of the language? And why did she always have to put a colon before every dollar figure? There was something cold, almost threatening about those two little dots. And another thing: the first letter had come from "E***, Inc.", while this one showed "E***, Ltd." It's like the company was setting up shop in the Virgin Isles or something, the better to launder my infrequent payments. But they still had a mailing address in Bethesda? *Missouri*?

This one got me kind of fired up, and that very night I sat down at the kitchen table and pulled out my stationery. It had been a while since I'd had any regular correspondence, so I guess I'd been saving up my energy.

Dear Natasha,

How nice to hear from you again. I hope you are well? I am well, too, thank you. It's a little chilly here, but not too bad. In fact, it's in weather like this that I say, "Thank God for gas and electric companies!" I really do. You people do important work, I don't deny it.

That said, I'm afraid there has been some small misunderstanding. You seem to have latched onto that Mr./Mrs. thing in my last letter (thank you so much!), but actually the most important part was the bit about my having already paid my bill. I'm sure you'll recall the photostatic copy of the check that I sent? It was a pretty good likeness of the real thing.

I'd be ever so grateful if you could clear this up for me. I think "clearing it up" would include removing the late fee and the interest charge as well, since I actually paid on time.

I guess that's about it. Oh, one last thing: I think you should look at Strunk and White about your use of articles. They're killers, I know.

Yours, etc.

Out it went with the morning's mail.

I'm embarrassed to admit it, but after that I started looking forward to brown envelopes in the mail. I mean, it's not like I have no personal life, but I was between girlfriends at the time, and my evenings were not exactly full. At the office I was fine; I could lose myself in paperwork as well as the next guy. But by the end of each afternoon I'd start wondering about the mail. Anticipation would grow as I left the office in the evening, and while I rode home on the bus I'd think, "Maybe today?" Silly, really—like a retiree hoping for a sweepstakes, or a writer waiting for a letter of acceptance from a magazine. Ridiculous. But that's the way it was.

It took a full two weeks for Natasha to write back to me. Perhaps she was distraught by the complexity of my situation. Or maybe she'd had a hard time deciding how to express her thoughts. How many times did she begin to write, only to set down the pen—or mouse, or whatever—bite her lower lip, and reconsider her response?

In the end, though, she found the words. They went something like this:

E***, Ltd.
P.O. Box 28271
Bethesda, MO 42002
THIRD NOTICE

Dear Mr. <Name>,

Thank you for your recent payment in the amount of: <AMOUNT1> for your overdue billing. However, please note that your late charges and penalty are still outstanding, and we require the full payment of: <AMOUNT2> no later than <DATE1>. Note that we have now written you <NUMBER1> times about this issue, and if it is not resolved quickly, we will be forced to close your account.

We value you as a customer, and we hope

If you wish to dispute this billing, please respond to

the address above, or contact your service agent at the number below.

Yours sincerely,

Natasha Naranski
Customer Service Representative
721-9394

So heartening, and yet so maddening! So close and yet so far! She'd unearthed my payment, my blessed Natasha (or had it just entered their system?)—and yet now she insisted on the payment of late charges I had not incurred. With one hand she caressed, while with the other she sank in her nails. It was *odi et amo*, I hate and I love—that old poetry all over again. And yet, and yet.... There was that strangely cantilevered sentence with the fragment *and we hope*, dangling without any punctuation at all, defying anyone to put a full stop to it. It seemed the very essence of open-ended aspiration and hopefulness. But that not-so-veiled threat! They may have written me NUMBER1 times about this, but it was starting to smell like a NUMBER2 to me.

The whole thing was tantalizing: just when I thought my messages were falling on deaf ears (or landing in some office for lost mail), some small detail would suggest communication had been established. Which was it?

I was restless in bed that night, unable to get the last letter out of my mind. I tossed and turned, turned and tossed. Finally I threw off the covers, plodded into the kitchen, and wrote Natasha in the wee hours while the cat prowled about my feet.

Dear Natasha,

Do you know the story of Pyramus and Thisbe? It's an old tale about two lovers who lived side by side but could never see each other because of the wall that separated their gardens. Instead, they sent messages through a crack in the wall. It wasn't what you'd call perfect communication, but it was better than nothing, and usually they got the gist of what each other was saying. When they were not able to be together, they comforted themselves by looking at the moon from their separate gardens, knowing they both shared that lunar spectacle, each of them unseen by the other.

I hope you will not think me forward if I compare our exchanges to those of Pyramus and Thisbe. My point is really that, even with the best of intentions, Pyramus and Thisbe ended up misunderstanding each other, with rather tragic consequences. (It was all a terrible mix-up, including a lion and a veil. I believe there was a dagger involved, too, but I'll spare you the details.)

All of this to say that I feel we are quite close to understanding one another on the matter of my payments, and yet so very far away. I am glad that you have recovered my initial payment, but surely this means you know that the check I sent arrived on time, and that no late charges thus apply? Besides, because your letter refers to the amount owed only as a kind of cipher—a mysterious "AMOUNT2"—I would not be able to pay even if I wanted to, which I do not.

I don't mind pointing out that this situation reminds me a lot of the conversations I used to have with my former girlfriend, which perhaps explains the "former" part. Couldn't we try a tiny bit harder? I'm confident that with one last push, we can break through the final barriers. We should both be able to get what we want, if only we can express our desires clearly. (If, indeed, one can ever know one's own desires!)

Wishing you

Yours, etc.

It was four in the morning by the time I finished, and despite my fatigue I thought it was a pretty good letter. Direct and yet friendly. Well, perhaps not friendly. More like compassionate. It's hard to strike just the right tone, and I suppose all attempts at communication with our fellow human beings are flawed somewhere. Take that open-ended "wishing you" part at the end of my note: it was my attempt to match the brilliant flourish of Natasha's "and we hope," and I left it in even though it didn't really work. It felt derivative.

Anyway, into the mail it went.

Several days passed. And then a week. And another. We left November behind, heading for mid-December, and still no word from Natasha. Had I gone too far? Had I said something I shouldn't have? I found myself going over the copy of my last letter (yes, I kept copies), tormented by what I'd said. Or left unsaid. Perhaps Pyramus and Thisbe wasn't the right story to tell? Maybe she was puzzling over that last line, wondering what, exactly, I wished her?

I wished her to write back, that's what I wished. It was pretty simple.

But more days passed, and after a while I no longer felt any thrill of anticipation as I reached into the box for my mail. Still, I picked through the envelopes and flyers obsessively, like a drug addict looking for a last hit that he knows damn well is not there. I was without hope, and yet unable to stop.

It was the day before Christmas when I received the last one. The familiar brown envelope lay in my trembling fingers. Same plastic window, same little smudges. It was a feeling akin to relief that I experienced, and I let the letter sit unopened on the kitchen table while I made a fresh pot of coffee. There was an effervescent pleasure to delaying the moment—now that I had the letter within reach. All in good time, all in good time, I thought to myself. Eventually I settled into the living room armchair, a cup of coffee at my side, the cat on my lap, and I gently slit the long seam of the envelope:

E***, Ltd.
P.O. Box 28271

Bethesda, MO 42002
FINAL NOTICE

Dear Mr. <Name>,

We have asked repeatedly (<DATE1>, <DATE2>, <DATE3>) for you to pay your outstanding balance of: <AMOUNT1>. Currently, this balance remains unpaid, and we have no choice but to refer your account to collections.

Moreover, we are now required to close account. Please be aware that your gas and electric service will be cancelled as of <DATE4>.

If you wish to dispute this billing, please respond to the address above, or contact your service agent at the number below.

Yours sincerely,

Irina Golosenko
Customer Service Representative
721-9394

Irina Golosenko? What had become of Natasha? Had she simply passed my file to a friend in the next cubicle? Had forces beyond her control interfered with her wish to respond? Or had E*** simply transferred her to a new division? In any case, communication had ground to a halt, and I confess to feeling somewhat jilted. Pyramus and Thisbe, indeed.

It is now approaching the New Year, and every day when I come home I expect the lights to be out, the heat off. If it doesn't happen today, it will be tomorrow. If not tomorrow, the day after.

∫

THE
DEATH
BUTTON

FALLING IN LOVE was never the plan. Far from it. For one thing, romance was beyond my means.

This was in college, back in the Dark Ages, long before people took out second mortgages on their homes or signed life insurance policies on expendable relatives just to finance an education. Costs were lower, yes, but disposable income is never more than a slight skin around the body of a budget, expanding and contracting with the organism, never thickening. Back then just buying groceries proved a challenge.

Drinking was easier—you merely had to separate wants from needs.

I was putting myself through school, living in a cramped apartment where I slept on a mattress stuffed halfway under a desk. Across from the bed a louver door opened directly into a tiny chamber between two bedrooms, a shared pass-through closet that my apartment-mate accessed through a second louver door on her side.

That's right: *her*. Michelle Hunter was a pretty girl with long hair and quiet charm, toiling to join the ranks of elementary school teachers. After her best friend dropped out, she needed someone to share the rent. And the closet.

Those louver doors, they were like the entrance to the magical wardrobe of *The Chronicles of Narnia*, except that instead of some religious allegory it was a world of very different passions that pulsed on the other side of the portal each time Michelle's boyfriend, a first-year medical student named Brad, spent the night. The closet served as an echo chamber, the louvers leading to the lovers, tuning me in to their amplified antics while I lay half-enclosed in the hollow under my desk like some mournful crustacean.

I didn't know what Brad had to offer that I didn't—aside from money and a future. And those chiseled good looks. Girls can be so picky.

Still, Michelle and I were just roommates, you see, albeit friendly ones. She liked to bake, and on Friday nights, while listening to loudspeakers belch music from the lawns of Fraternity Row, she'd wipe floury wisps of hair out of her eyes and I'd grease the cookie sheets. She taught me how to make a Bundt cake, but as far as I was concerned her pastime could just as well have been embalming. *What do you say we pump formaldehyde into a corpse tonight*, she could have proposed, and I'd have mashed my hands together with glee. One night she taught me how to knead bread, guiding my hands, our fingers meeting and mixing in the dough. Before the pans had even gone into the oven, something inside of me had already been seared.

While the loaves or batter baked, the apartment still reeking of yeast, I would read Michelle passages from my current classes—a few saucy verses of Middle English, something prim and pointed from Jane Austen, or a canto of Dante. If I waxed sufficiently melodramatic, I could get her to laugh.

At night we were separated by the hollowness of the closet, the louvers screening light like the lashes of half-opened eyes. When I extinguished my own lamp—which I hastened to do, wearied by baking—I could sometimes watch stripes of Michelle's silhouette moving across the double filter of the doors.

My problem was the rent. But also Brad. So two problems. And they were somehow related, Brad and money, because he had a lot of it. It made you wonder why Michelle wasn't going over to his place all the time. Who knows? Maybe he was practicing making house calls. Maybe he just wanted to keep her at arm's length. Maybe there were other women.

In any case, he had nice stuff. One day he pulled up in a brand new BMW.

"Wow. Nice ride," I told him.

"325i," he replied. "High performance. Five-speed transmission."

He had nothing on me: I had a *ten* speed. It was a Schwinn.

He tossed me the keys. "Hey, English Major. You should probably get used to parking other people's cars. Betcha five bucks you can't even figure out how to start it."

Hilarious. Just the kind of budding doctor you'd want to entrust your life to. Still, I wasn't above taking his money. In Humanities 101 we'd learned about Pascal's famous wager—the what-do-you-have-to-lose argument for believing in God—and my first bet with Brad smacked of just such certainty. Unfortunately, Pascal hadn't had to deal with the ignition gimmickry of German engineering. There was a special trick I couldn't figure out, and my wallet ended up shedding its last five-dollar bill.

Often Brad would come over with a skeletal hand or foot or other fragment of the human form—sometimes models that came apart like children's puzzles, sometimes the preserved genuine article. Recently he'd brought us a human skull, which took up residence on the kitchen table. I named him Yorick, and every morning while I ate my Fruit Loops, this cranial companion grinned at me expectantly, as though begging for a bite.

In theory our medical student was supposed to study these show-and-tell pieces to learn all their bits and names, but mostly his study of the human body at our apartment began and ended with Michelle. In all those months I never saw him crack open a book. One morning I asked about this, pointing out how some of us dedicated long nights to dense pages.

"Yeah, well," he replied, "I guess that shows that some people are slow learners, doesn't it?" Another knee-slapper. But by the time I'd crafted a comeback, he'd left the room.

The only good thing about Brad's insults were the shy looks Michelle slipped me in their wake—an act of sympathy that encouraged me to angle for his scorn. I responded to her with my patented hangdog expression. One evening I tried to pry a bit while she mixed cookie dough, but Michelle just nibbled at her lip and refused to criticize her beau. This loyalty endeared her to me all the more, but it didn't further my cause.

But what were we to do? She was trapped. Or I was trapped.

We were all trapped. It was as confining as the tomb-like bed under the table in my room, where I knocked my head every time I jolted awake to eerie sounds hooting through that closet.

There were a few mild concussions.

Did I mention the louver doors yet?

The apartment should have been cheap. It was tiny, in poor repair, and fell short of the electrical codes of any modern nation. But we were in a seller's market, and I found myself dipping into next term's tuition money just to pay my rent. The dwindling of my finances required action. If nothing changed, I'd soon have to move out and leave Michelle to Brad. On campus I'd been on the lookout for a job, starting with ambition, seeking a position that would pay me to sit at a desk and do my homework, interrupting my reading once every leap year to check out a book or answer a phone. But coveted positions like this had been monopolized by bewitching girls—full-fledged women, really, by the looks of them—hired as decorative pieces by male superiors at the library or departmental offices.

Desperation is the mother of invention, and that's how I started selling my body. No, I don't mean some cheap and tawdry sex trade, a bargain-basement gigolo. I mean the real thing: *selling* my *body*—as in, *Here's my spleen, how much do you want for it?* It was a principle taught me by the Tooth Fairy, that dainty pixie of dental prostitution who had demonstrated in my youth that pieces of me were worth cold, hard cash. Maybe it was Brad who triggered this inspiration, thanks to the chunks of human skeleton that kept appearing *chez moi*. Maybe I should have offered him a commission—Brad, my body-parts impresario.

Back then selling yourself was an innovative undertaking—years before people started waking up in bathtubs full of crushed ice after a roofie-laced drink, the left side of their lower backs feeling tender and light.

There were a lot of ways to go about it, and I followed the principle I'd learned from selling an old bike after high school. Barely operational, the Raleigh had been worth about fifteen bucks on the open market, though I found I could sell the front wheel for five, the back for ten, the chain for two, the seat for three, and the frame for seven. I even traded the bell for a parakeet. It was often best to sell things in parts, and that was the approach I took, starting by hawking my lifeblood.

This transaction took place in a seedy part of town not far from our ramshackle neighborhood. Truth be told, it wasn't all of my blood they wanted, just the yellow, urine-like stuff they could extract from it. That was the great puzzle: blood you had to donate, but plasma, which involved a much more complicated process, you could sell for twenty-five bucks a pint. The price has gone up since, but back then such a figure was nothing to sneeze at, although sneeze I did, violently, as the lightheadedness from my second weekly visit triggered tickles in my nose.

The plasma center was like the closet between my bedroom and Michelle's—a porous membrane at the juncture of two worlds. This one attracted winos and bums staggering in to finance their next bender, bringing them in contact with impoverished students. That first day I hopped up on a cot next to a three hundred pound vagrant who looked like a stunt double for Walt Whitman—except that his nose was veined with purple and the beard was clotted with what appeared to be bits of partially digested fettuccine. He also had a needle in his arm, but that didn't keep him from scrutinizing my arrival, studying me while I rolled up a sleeve for my deflowering. The nurse swabbed my arm, then skewered the crook of my elbow with all the gentleness of an innkeeper whacking a spigot into the bunghole of a keg. My vital fluids began to drain through plastic tubes, and I lifted my book with feigned nonchalance. Old Walt leaned over and stared hard and close, as if meaning to count my nose hairs. The sourness of his breath, a generous burp of which he shared, suggested we might soon see more of his vomitous emissions. Leaves of grass indeed. It was at that moment, when we met eye to eye in the clinic, that I inquired about how often he frequented the establishment.

He squinted at the volume of T. S. Eliot's *Wasteland* in my hands. "I read that once," he rumbled. His cheeks bulged, and with considerable exertion he suppressed a new gastric eruption. "I thought it needed editing."

Thirty minutes later I was buttoned up and heading out, a twenty-dollar bill and five singles alive in my pocket. I hadn't told Michelle about this particular venture, but suddenly my future looked bright—and also a little blurry, for about an hour.

I didn't care. The money rounded out my month, helping to keep me in the apartment, only a closet away from Michelle.

Plasma was a good deal. You could sell it twice a week, which was almost enough time for your body to keep up with production. I'd turned my circulatory system into a kind of ATM, and although my grade point average took a hit because of my occasional afternoon blackouts, I looked for other parts of my body to sell as well. Especially useful were things that regenerated, for they represented a smarter long-term business plan. Fantine had sold her locks in *Les Misérables*, so why not me? It turned out that good hair could fetch a few hundred bucks, even more if it was pure—untouched by dyes, straighteners, or other chemicals. My head sported a mop in its most virgin state, rarely even tainted by shampoo. Still, a head of hair was like a savings bond—it took a long time to mature—and the more often I checked in the mirror the slower the whole business seemed to go.

I needed to diversify, and what was diversification if not a kind of dissemination? There was a sperm bank not too far away, and that could pay big bucks. White gold. I applied immediately, but apparently my quality didn't match my enthusiasm. Breast milk had a market price, but I wasn't lactating.

Then in one of my classes we read *Prometheus Bound*, and while I didn't catch all the subtleties of sly old Aeschylus, I got the big picture. Prometheus was an asshole of the first order, kind of an Olympian version of Brad. But his punishment interested me: an eagle swooped down and gobbled up his liver every day, the organ growing back overnight.

It turns out that the liver *does* regenerate. Some people prefer to call it compensatory growth, and you have to be careful not to take too much. And when you cut out a lobe, try not to interfere with the biliary tree because that can turn into a real mess.

I studied this one pretty closely. The liver's kind of an important body part, so you don't want to screw it up.

As an English major I didn't feel like I'd learned anything in particular during my first three years, but my advisor said I was learning how to learn, and wasn't that the gift of a liberal arts education. So I studied the liver with more gusto than I gave to Chaucer, with the kind of passion I found only in Shakespeare. The more I read, the more I marveled. The liver is *life*, a mystical organ, a magical chamber within the body, transmuting all manner of fluids into gold. It makes bile to help with digestion, and it generates proteins. It contributes to the very plasma that was nourishing my rent. But most of all, it detoxifies the blood, filtering out pollutants the way Michelle sifted away clots of flour, or the way the slats of the louver doors screened light from her bedroom, like the louver-liver ducts of my imagination that strained out impurities like Brad. What could it not do, this organ of perfection, this metabolic maestro? The heart and lungs get all the publicity, but if it's moody complexity you're after, look to the liver.

Anyhow, I got all the details. Anything you want to know about lobes, peritoneal ligaments or celiac ganglia, I'm your man.

One evening I dozed off in front of the TV and Michelle overheard my passed-out mumblings, from which she deduced I'd been peddling my plasma. She jabbed me awake and pressed for details. Brad joined the conversation, pointing out that leaving my body to science could net a few hundred bucks paid in advance. The glint in his eye was worrisome, as though he might aim his BMW to hasten my donation. He volunteered that there was a black market for extra kidneys and other things we happen to have in duplicate.

"You could part with half your brain," he quipped, proposing another wager. "I'll bet you five bucks you're only using one hemisphere anyway. Of course, there's really only one way to prove it."

This would have been our second bet. Michelle gritted her teeth, but she didn't need to worry. I'd already put my one hemisphere to work and decided it wasn't worth the money to sacrifice the other.

It turned out not to matter, because in the end I landed my dream job. There were medical research teams on campus—even

Brad knew about this—and they paid fifty to a hundred bucks to anyone willing to pump himself full of trial medications. Technically you weren't supposed to participate in more than one study at a time, though I had a tradition of holding down multiple jobs. But it turns out the side effects can be a lot worse when your body is already low on plasma. You get pretty woozy. Trust me on that one.

Then I learned about the projects being done in the Psych Department, mostly by graduate students desperate for data for their dissertations. It was the perfect solution: all I had to do was let them think they were playing with my mind while I nudged test results in their favor. As soon as I figured out what they wanted to prove, I aimed to please, performing their word tests and puzzles in ways that would confirm the wildest hypotheses. It felt good to participate in the advance of science.

Then a new fad swept through the department and test subjects were being outfitted with mechanical counters: you pushed a button and the number on the counter clicked up a step. They used these for all sorts of experiments. How often do people nap during the day? Take a counter and push the button every time you wake up. How often do you drink alcohol? Push the button with each glass. How often do you experience déjà vu? How many times do you find yourself daydreaming? With what frequency do you think of home? How often do you experience déjà vu? How often do you find yourself the victim of a cheap joke? Click, click, click—people would push the button.

The test I really wanted was also the most popular: How often do you think about sex? I had it all worked out: I was going to punch it up to thirteen on the first day, and after the two-week test period, when I handed it in, I'd explain that I'd topped the counter out at 10,000, and it was on the second round. But everyone wanted the Sex Button, and I didn't get in, despite my excellent reputation for producing desired results. Maybe it was because of my sperm. Did I mention that I also had a number of concussions?

Since I didn't get the Sex Button, I got the next best thing: the Death Button. Officially it was the Mortality Consciousness Test, the MCT—kind of a morbid version of the ACT with a single question: How often do you think about The End—you know, kicking the bucket, croaking, meeting your maker, biting the big one, pushing up daisies, going out feet-first. At the outset I wasn't so keen, but then I realized that this was even slicker than the Sex Button. I could leave the counter zeroed out and get paid for nothing. I wouldn't even have to lie. After all, I was twenty years old. Why would I waste my time thinking about the back door to my life when I was barely in the front lobby? Sure, you might argue, it's all linked together. But still.

The experiment was simple in design, and over the course of two weeks it would net me a hundred bucks. All I had to do was click the button every time I imagined my own expiration. There were several of us at the training session, a room full of potential lemmings. I skipped out early because of my appointment at the plasma center, a stop that left me pleasantly groggy. Almost tipsy. It was Walt Whitman stretched out next to me again, and afterward I wondered if the nurse hadn't switched the tubes somehow, giving me my neighbor's inebriated blood instead. I was going to ask him if he'd noticed a mix-up, but he was snoring pretty loudly.

All in all it had been a decent week. I already had my share of the rent for Michelle, and I hadn't seen Brad in a while. The closet had been awfully quiet of late, and I'd started wondering if he was still in the picture. Maybe Michelle was now available. Maybe she'd turned him out because I'd turned her on. Maybe she was just waiting for me to ask. Maybe she'd been pining away in her own demure fashion. Such were the thoughts my plasma-free state induced in the one hemisphere of my brain Brad said I used. Besides, no one could deny it was technically possible for Michelle to fall for me, and that very idea put a spring in my pedaling as I cruised home on my Schwinn.

I was rolling down the street that cut through campus—late afternoon with a lot of people milling about—when a squirrel appeared out of nowhere. It was a suicide move, a kamikaze rodent throwing himself under the wheels of a bicycle. But then, at the last second, he lost his resolve and hesitated, as though wondering if, despite all the evidence to the contrary, he still had something to live for. Meanwhile, I was careening toward him. All the little guy had to do was decide: should he leap back to safety, or charge along on the same course to the other side? If he zigged, I could zag, and we'd both get through it in one piece. Forward or back, either way he'd be fine. But instead he chose option C, the in-between choice of not choosing. He twitched forward, stopped, arched his back as if he were turning around, and froze again. He didn't look up at me, but by the way his ears shivered, you knew that he knew what was happening.

It was the smallest of bumps, the kind of bounce you get from going over a ridge of dirt, but this one came with a crack like the snapping of a twig. Before I could even react, I'd gone right over my nut-eating friend, and I turned in time to see the last furry spasm. So eager, so beady-eyed just moments before, and now he was meat, some of his innards squished out through his open mouth.

It took a minute before I fully absorbed the scene. Then, as if subject to a hypnotic force, I reached into my jacket pocket, withdrawing a metal object in my fist. The Death Button. I stared at the counter, at the squirrel, and then at my thumb as it reached over and pressed the button. The tumbler quivered, quivered, and the mechanism clicked: 0001.

That was how it started. An accident. I'd witnessed a squirrel take the plunge, and my wincing triggered a contraction that extended down my arm all the way to the thumb curled over the Death Button. I'd identified with that little fellow and his indecision. Squirrels, I'd seen, are mortal. The rodent had been ferried across the river Styx. It had squeezed through the portal between life and death. Its organs were now disorganized. It had shed its mortal coil.

I felt the breath of the Reaper on the back of my neck, as sour as Walt Whitman's. Before I knew it, I had pressed the button again: 0002.

I could have *not* pressed it. There was no God of Psychology looking over my shoulder, requiring that I record these sentiments. But I pressed it all the same. As if I had no choice, like when your number comes up—a thought that led me to press it again. It was crazy. I'd gone for twenty years ignoring death with great panache, but now here I was, my brain entertaining the idea that I might not be long for this world. Which required me to click it again. And again.

I knew how this worked. We'd learned about it in my Physics-for-English-Majors class—the uncertainty principle, the idea that the presence of the observer can change the result of the experiment. As soon as a device was introduced to register my thoughts, it didn't just record them: it *produced* them. Somebody mentions a *Death Button*, and it's hard to think of anything else. Carrying one in your pocket makes you want to push it, and pushing it makes you think about what it means, and thinking about what it means leads to the desire to push it again.

Then I realized I'd not actually been so free of morbid thoughts in the past. Back when I was twelve, there'd been the day I understood that science wouldn't lick the mortality problem in time for my generation—an awareness I squeezed out of my consciousness by focusing on other urges that were starting to bloom within me. But even more recently, images worthy of Death-Button-pushing had nibbled at the edges of my life. Whenever I pumped out plasma, for example. Or every time I saw Walt Whitman and wondered if one day he'd stop showing up at the center. Or when I spooned up my cereal in the company of Brad's pal Yorick at the breakfast table. Or if I read a book for an English class, which were all pretty damned macabre when you got right down to it.

The Death Button no longer seemed like such a hot idea for raising capital. Maybe I should have just sold my liver after all. Not all of it, mind you—just a Couinaud segment or two, like the caudate lobe, something I could spare, as long as there weren't any complications during the operation. The thought of which made me click the button again.

Less than one post-squirrel hour had elapsed, and already I'd reached three digits on the counter, at which point I was ready to declare a moratorium on button-pushing—a word that made me want to click again. But should I? I found myself faced with a conundrum. Let's say you imagine something—ketchup, for example—and then two minutes later ketchup crosses your mind again. Is that a new thought, or just a continuation, after commercial interruption? And while we're at it, what's the difference between a thought and a feeling, between a vague impression and a reverie? If you make up a list of condiments for your shopping list, and you think, *Hey, we need some ketchup*, that's a bona fide thought. It's not necessarily brooding—you're not obsessed with ketchup or anything—but no one will deny you've *thought* about it. But let's say you walk into a Burger King, and you notice an aroma but don't put a word to it. If that happened in the midst of a Ketchup Consciousness Test—a KCT—would you push the counter for it?

The ketchup example was a useful distraction—until I considered how the sauce is also used outside the realm of fast food, how it can substitute for other fluids in plays or movies. It's not perfect blood—it doesn't have any plasma and it hasn't been detoxified by the liver—but those little pouches of paste explode convincingly when someone fires a handgun on stage.

The image warranted another push of the Button.

That evening things went from bad to worse. Brad was there, his BMW parked at an angle outside our building. Inside he was in prime form. Yorick the skull was still with us, sitting in the kitchen, grinning at all who passed by. I reached discreetly into my pocket and clicked away to my heart's discontent.

I locked myself in my room and tried to think pleasant thoughts, all of them inevitably curving back to Inevitable. The counter was climbing. What good did it do for me to trade bits of my body for cash, to tank up on chemicals, or let people play with my mind? Why bother sneaking glances at Michelle when Brad wasn't looking? It would all be over soon enough. What are we in the end but indecisive squirrels scurrying for treasures we will hide and forget? Or imminent cranial decorations destined for breakfast tables in other kitchens in other eras?

That night, stretched out on my mattress in the dark, I listened to Brad boinking Michelle on the other side of the louvers. At first it was clear she didn't want to. I heard the whispered protests, and then his plaintive insistence. I was rooting for her, but eventually she caved, and Brad set himself in motion, the bed groaning with every thrust, faster and faster. He was the BMW of lovers—high speed with good acceleration, and no use for brakes whatsoever. It all seemed deadly somehow. Click, click, click.

The next morning, Brad was drinking coffee from my special mug, his feet up on the only other chair at the kitchen table, the Sunday funnies open in his lap. Michelle was cutting fruit at the counter. And me? I'd not slept a wink, running the counter up to great heights, hitting four digits. My knees wobbled from the shortage of plasma. It was Michelle who begged Brad to take his feet off the other chair.

"I was just reading about you," he said, waving the funnies in my face. He'd opened it to Beetle Bailey.

Yorick smiled at me from the table—a skull after my own heart, a happy-go-lucky cranium without a worry in the world. It was like a Renaissance painting: some guy in a flowing bathrobe sits down at a banquet table to have his Cheerios, and there's a *memento mori* there as his pal.

Eat, drink, and be merry.

That skull and I, we'd grown close.

I didn't even need to leave the room to record my thoughts. I had the counter right there in my pocket.

When I edged Yorick away from my orange juice, Brad barked at me to leave him alone, and when I didn't cease fast enough, he swatted at me with the newspaper, sending our friendly ball of bone on a wobbly roll off the edge of the table, smashing on the tile. I looked down to find teeth, occipital plates and pieces of mandible scattered across the floor. It was all over. My breakfast companion was gone. Alas, poor Yorick! We'd known him well.

"Look what you've done, you idiot," Brad cried. He said it was medical school property. Actually, he referred to it as *goddamn medical school shit*, and called me a *fuckhead* to boot. That was his *homework*, he said, and I'd screwed it up. I was going to have to pay.

So there I was, contemplating my own mortality and secretly wishing for Brad's, all the while clicking away on the Death Button, when an amazing thing happened—as when a louvered door opens, or the clouds part and a goddess speaks from the sky.

It was Michelle's voice, coming out in her tiniest Michelle whisper.

"You weren't exactly *using* that skull, were you?" she murmured.

You could barely hear the hint of reproach, but it was there all right, like a blip on a seismograph. Something in the ground had shifted.

Brad noticed it too, and he studied her. We both did. That look in Michelle's eyes, the mix of panic and indecision, it was familiar to me, I'd seen it before, just the other day on the face of my furry friend as I bore down on him with my Schwinn.

If there was a chance Michelle might break free of Brad's bonds and make a run for it, I wanted to be of service. However, I'd also wanted to help that squirrel, and look how that turned out. You have to tread carefully in this world, or else people who don't deserve it get tire tracks all over their spine. But what exactly are you supposed to do? I was ready to jump in, willing to do my part. I just needed to know which way Michelle was going to go. Would she zig or would she zag?

And that's when it came to me, the lesson, the epiphany, the revelation: *You can't ever wait for the squirrel.*

I must have said that out loud, because now Brad turned to me. "What the fuck?"

I followed up on Michelle's question, asking Brad if he actually needed Yorick anymore. After all, he'd claimed to be such a quick study. Surely he had mastered all the parts long ago?

Just uttering those words did wonders. I felt like that ape at the beginning of *2001*, the weak guy who picks up a femur from a pile of bones, finding that it fits his hand just right. And then he starts to smash things with it. Preternatural Yoricks.

Brad's eyes went small. What was I implying, he wanted to know.

Any other day I'd have backed off. But for the past twenty-four hours death had become my constant companion, and as all the philosophers will tell you, that's the only true way to prepare yourself for your final hour. Plus, I was sleep-deprived. And overdrawn on my plasma account.

Which is how we got into another wager. Brad sneered in his charming way, claiming he'd already learned more about human anatomy than I would ever know. He bet me ten bucks he could beat me in a quiz on the body, on any part I wanted. He stuck out his hand to shake on it.

I admit it was tempting. There I was, chronically underfunded, with Brad offering me another opportunity to gamble. But, in fact, it's not worth taking chances unless the stakes are high enough, unless it's something you really want, and I told him so.

"Twenty bucks," he spat out, doubling the pot. "Fifty."

I turned him down. The sums were both too little and too much, more than I could afford, and also strangely off the mark, like it was all the wrong currency. Then I realized what I wanted more than anything else. It wasn't Yorick off my breakfast table, or even next month's rent. What I wanted was Brad out of my apartment. Out of my life.

Yes, that was it. I felt like a peasant who'd just realized how nicely a nobleman's head would fit at the end of his pike.

Brad had a good chuckle when I proposed that wager, though it kind of dried in his throat when Michelle didn't smile.

"You're on, English Major," he said. "But if I win, then it's *you* that gets the boot. You clear out. Today. This morning. You're history."

Touching Brad wasn't one of my favorite activities, but I shook his hand.

"OK, pinhead," he smiled after we'd settled the formalities. "What'll it be? Skeletal? Muscular? Cardiovascular?" His mouth caressed the names of the bodily systems.

Even if English majors mostly learn useless fluff, every now and then you get a chance to trot out a parlor trick.

"If you don't mind," I told him, "I'm more of an internal organ man, myself. I've always had a soft spot for the liver."

* * *

Brad moved his gear out that afternoon, taking the pieces of Yorick with him. In some ways, I think he was glad to be gone. Michelle's period of mourning for that particular relationship was abridged, and soon thereafter our courtship began. We baked together on Friday evenings. I learned how to make scones. Not long after, I landed a job and stopped selling myself. And then one night my universe expanded: Michelle opened the louver doors on her side, and she invited me through.

THE
VISIT

THEY'D MISSED THE TURN outside the village and crossed the river at the wrong bridge. The wife had trouble following the map, and by the time the husband pointed the car onto the dirt drive that snaked up the hill through the mist, they were already thirty minutes late, their young son nearly carsick from the overlong ride, or else from the bickering.

Outbuildings appeared in the clearing, great hulks looming behind threads of fog. They stepped out of the car onto sodden ground as their friends emerged from the stone house. Soon it was hugs and handshakes, the hosts holding the boy's narrow shoulders to get a look at him, asking if he remembered them from before— although no, of course he wouldn't, it was too long ago, wasn't it? They re-introduced him to their daughter, a touch younger and serious, the grim but dazzling fairy of this rugged yard that leaked right into the surrounding forest, whereas the boy had only ever known flat and groomed lawns, most of them fenced.

There was still light, so the guests, who more than anything wished for a drink, received instead a tour. The visitors admired the sagging barn, its floor rotted, the wood of its doors soft. In one corner the girl prodded a pulpy mass with a wand-like twig, revealing a teeming ball of grubs that made the boy gape and the mother shudder.

The sloping yard bled with wetness. Dew wicked from the grass into the veined soil, capillaries of moisture weeping into dribbles, dribbles pulsing into trickles, trickles into rivulets, all seeping toward a pool of black water thirty feet across. A pond. In the middle a huddle of mallards congregated, keeping their distance from a gray goose. And if all this weren't enough to make the city boy marvel, there were also frogs in the grass, slim speckled ones that jumped just as he closed his hands around them, making him giggle and chase them in fits and starts to the water's edge, where he probed with a stick. The mother warned about the slickness, the mud, but the husband cut her off, telling her to let the boy be, just for once.

Dragged inside, the children feigned patience while drinks were served and crackers traveled on a tray. The conversation lagged after the flurry of newness, the four adults nodding and smiling, each trying to recall why the four of them used to get along so well, and then, with the help of the Chablis, remembering, so that the conversation crackled anew. This cued the children's disappearance into the hallway. Reports continued among the grown-up—the essentials about jobs and schools, a few anecdotes—but soon they circled back to what had bound them, the outings of years ago, long before the arrival of kids, especially the summer when they'd vacationed together in the mountains, renting that A-frame cabin, the two couples playing at a simple life that one of them would end up taking seriously. Oh, and then the fish story—not of catching, but of cooking, and once again the husbands grinned their way through the ritual humiliation of its recounting.

As dinner approached, the children were to be fetched from whatever nook they'd scurried to, which provided the opportunity to lead the guests upstairs, to finish the tour and show them the room they would occupy for the night.

In her bedroom they found the girl lying on her stomach, feet knocking together in the air as she turned the pages of the book.

No, she said blankly. She had no idea where the boy had gone. She'd been reading alone for some time now.

They checked the other bedrooms and the office. Nor was he to be found in the bathroom. He couldn't be far, the hosts joked, the house wasn't that big. The mother called the boy's name as she sailed down the stairs, the first creep of urgency in her voice. After the kitchen and dining room, she paused in the hallway, feeling a draft, almost a current, at her back. She turned: the front door stood ajar.

One by one they filed into the fogged darkness, scanning the oddly shrouded stumps and uneven ground, their eyes keen for movement. The hosts, less easy now, called the boy's name as well, stepping into the cavernous barn and the shed, one of them returning to the house for flashlights. The father moved briskly, his cries blunted by the damp.

The mother began in one direction, then another, then a third, panting, her shoes smacking with suction in the muck. A ball formed in her chest, and the treetops began to dance. Something darted underfoot and she gasped as a frog flew, landing in the tall grass two feet away before springing into the air once more, and she raised her eyes beyond the frog, tracing forward in the direction of its jumps, past the ducks who now stood on the ground, past the goose, her gaze drawn into a stain of blackness in the shadows, an opening in the surface of the grass.

It was the pond. Dark, quiet, implacable.

And when she parted her lips, as if to whisper a word, a name, everything inside her gave way.

* * *

How lumpy the yard was, the hostess exclaimed later as she helped her friend scrape drying mud from her jeans. Practically dangerous! She'd been after her husband to roll them a bit of lawn, because, really, you could see how people would lose their footing.

This came after the boy had turned up in the old pantry, asleep next to the cat, exhausted from the drive and the newness. His father made a show of scolding him, and after a silence that risked becoming too long, the other husband made the first joke, a feeble one, but that led to more talk as they moved to the dinner table. Kids used to run wild, someone said. But these days it's all play dates and art classes. What luck to have a hillside—practically a mountain—for a back yard! Don't you think? Don't you?

Yes, breathed the boy's mother, rejoining the conversation. What luck.

Voices grew loud as the platters circulated. The host topped off glasses of wine. And with lavish servings of words, always more words, they covered over the memory of the pond, black and still.

GENERAL
RELATIVITY

LET ME TELL YOU about the first time—the alpha experience, the egg, the seed, the source. Picture it. I'm on my way to California to troubleshoot a database system, sitting in a departure lounge at O'Hare, waiting for my flight to be called. To pass the time, I pick up a new novel by a writer I've never read. Let's call the author A, the book Z. So, I'm sitting there reading A's Z, and as the novel starts out we learn that the main character has just lost his whole family—his wife and two kids—in an airplane crash. They were traveling from Boston to Los Angeles, and the plane simply dropped from the air, it "fell out of the sky." That's how A put it.

It's nothing but a book, right? You feel kinda sorry for the guy, but hey, he's just a figment of A's imagination, so it doesn't stop me from doing what I need to do. I get a coffee from the Starbucks, along with an almond biscotti. I give my girlfriend a quick call. Then, before you know it, they're starting to board the aircraft. Eventually I get on, and there's still room for my bag in the overhead compartment and I have an aisle seat. Everything's cool. The plane takes off, and pretty soon we're thirty-five thousand feet up, cruising along.

So I pull out A's novel and start reading again, sinking into the world of the guy whose family *fell out of the sky*, and I think: "What a terrible book to read during a plane ride," along with a little follow-up: "especially on a flight to Los Angeles." You see, L.A. is where A's character's family was headed when they fell. True, they had left from Boston, while I just took off from Chicago, but still. Then, guess what? While I'm thinking about the trip to LAX in A's Z, our 727 hits an air pocket the size of Kansas. We drop a thousand feet, maybe more. Never felt anything like it before. The empty cup on my tray table actually hovers in the air, that's how fast we fall.

Some guy in the aisle floats up and bonks the ceiling, and everyone's screaming—for a couple of moments, anyway. The whole thing lasts only a few seconds, and soon the stewardesses are back again, wobbling up and down the aisle, smoothing down their skirts, trying hard not to look terrified. I can see in their eyes that none of them have experienced a fall like that before. It's a good thing they hadn't served dinner yet.

So what's the big deal, you ask? The big deal is that we had just lived through a miniature version of what I'd read about not half an hour earlier. The bigger deal was the thought that flashed through my mind: "This has happened before." No, I don't mean the déjà-vu-vague-sort-of-feeling that you've experienced something like this in the past. I mean, instead, the *Twilight Zone* kind of feeling, the one where you *know* something similar really has happened before. And I don't mean the falling out of the sky; I mean the sense that recently something else had happened to me after reading about it in a book. But I couldn't put my finger on it.

I know what you're thinking: it's a coincidence, the law of averages.

That's what I thought, too. After all, I work with computers. I know mathematics, along with all the twists and turns of probability. You can have repetition without a pattern. Just because you roll snake eyes twice in a row doesn't mean it's any more—or less—likely to come up again.

Two days later, on the way back from L.A, I decide to get a different book, by a different author. Just to play it safe. Let's call the new author B, and his book is *Y*. Well, wouldn't you know it? *Y* also starts with a plane. How did this happen? It's not like I go up to the girl at the airport book stand and ask her to recommend titles about air disasters. It's not like there's a special shelf marked Books You Don't Want to Read During your Flight. It just happens. So there we are, already in the air when I crack this one open. It starts with a plane crossing the night sky. The aircraft has been hijacked. A suicide bomber has wrapped himself in plastique. Before you know it, the plane is just a ball of fire against the dark of night.

Well, that was pretty gripping, and since I was on the red-eye flight, I could look out the window past the guy next to me and imagine what a fireball would look like against that deep, thick blue. The navigation light at the end of the wing flashed red, and each time it blinked it looked like a tiny burst of flame. In B's book the main character was watching the air disaster from the ground with a group of others, and there were a bunch of cries and shrieks. Some guy standing next to him said, "For the holy love of God," which strikes me as a little odd, a bit overdone. But what do I know? Some people say things like that and some don't. You have a choice. There's chocolate and vanilla.

I know what you're thinking: who *cares* what he said? No big deal. But actually, *yes big deal.*

Here's why. So I'd been reading B's book *Y*, and the whole thing made me think of that "coincidence" (your word, not mine) I'd had with A's book *Z*, where reality imitated the book. And I thought, I sure hope that doesn't happen again. The last thing I needed was for one of the passengers to get up and detonate himself, or set his tennis shoes on fire, or whatever. I could just picture our plane exploding, jet fuel searing the body parts, luggage flying like shrapnel. All that would remain is people's socks, underwear and shaving kits raining down on the population below. And I laughed. To myself, that is. I thought, Ha! What an *imagination.* And I went back to the book. Only to discover that in *Y* it turns out there *was* no terrorist, no fireball—it had all been in the narrator's imagination. Just like me—just the way I had imagined our own plane exploding

That weirded me out, so I put the book down for a while. But then a little while later the fellow sitting next to me, a guy I don't know from Adam, shifts in his seat. He's looking out the window, craning his neck to see to the east, and his face is glowing the color of bronze. "For the holy love of God," he mutters, and the hair on the back of my neck goes all tingly. I see that he sees that I heard him, and I say, "What's up?" And he says, "You should look out the window. It's like a ball of fire."

OK, OK. He wasn't talking about a plane. This was a red-eye flight, and as the sun came up, it did look rather like a ball of fire. But still. By that time I felt like I was sitting next to my goddamn double. The guy even looked like me. Well, he was about my age, at least.

To hell with probability: if you roll snake-eyes ten times in a row, something is haywire. So I started trying to figure out the pattern. What made this happen? Maybe it had to do with planes. Or with airport bookshops. I don't go in for the supernatural, but some part of me was thinking, maybe it's a message; maybe there's some connection between reading and flying. So over the next couple of days I ran some tests. I had a round trip to Minneapolis—short flights, but enough for a few air disaster stories. You wouldn't think tales like that would be easy to find, but it turns out there's a pile of them. It's like a whole genre. There was a crash landing in the Sierra Madre, a stormy flight over the Andes, a one-way bombing raid in WWII.

You might call it tempting fate, reading stories like that. But here's the thing: *nothing happened.* On the printed page planes went into death spirals, or lightning would fry the controls, and each time I got to one of these passages I'd check my seatbelt and make sure my tray table was in an upright position, bracing myself for the shock. I looked around at my fellow passengers—women bouncing babies, guys snoring, kids laying out playing cards—and I shook my head at their immense ignorance of what was about to befall us. But nothing did. Nothing befell. We took off, flew, and landed. End result: zilch. Perfectly normal. Smooth. Once we even landed on time.

Which proves what?

So I quit worrying about it.

Which is precisely when it happened again. And this time it had nothing to do with airplanes. I'd spent the day troubleshooting an installation on the north side of Chicago, tracking down a really pesky bug in a financial database, and I was taking a cab back home. There was a lot of traffic, so I settled back and started paging through a *Time* magazine the previous fare had abandoned in the back seat. I'll admit that I had a strange feeling—an eerie sensation of imminence—but I pushed it out of my mind. Among the news items of the world there was a little article about the recent rise of the opium trade. A squib at the bottom of a page. I guess in

Afghanistan there are boys and girls out there picking poppies to help mom and dad pay the bills, to make ends meet at the end of the month. And there was a snippet that talked about the history of opium, with a reference to a nineteenth-century book about opium eating by some English guy named Thomas de Quincey. I can't really just give this writer a letter (Q?) because the name is important. I didn't know the book or the author. Still, it was kind of interesting, although opium is not really my thing. Anyway, I had just read this passage in *Time* when the cab hit a pothole, and the bounce made me look up, and what did my eyes fall upon but the sign for a hole-in-the-wall bar called "De Quincey's Ale." With a big, green shamrock next to the name. The guy was an Englishman, so I don't know what the hell he was doing on the sign for an Irish pub.

That one really made me jump. I mean, the sign was pretty small, and it was on the other side of the street, hard to see even if you were expecting it. Had I lifted my head a second later, or had I pointed my nose three degrees to the left, I'd have missed it. But there it was. As if someone had placed it there just for me.

So my problem had nothing to do with plane travel. Maybe it was tied to public transportation? And it was not just books—even magazines were *Time* bombs, just waiting to go off. I felt like I was being stalked by printed matter, except that the words weren't sneaking up on me; they were in front. I mean, I would read something in a book or magazine, and then *voilà*, it would happen. The back of a cereal box could turn into a goddamned fortune cookie. And the events were occurring closer to my reading about them. Back when I noticed the thing with A's book, there had been a lag, a little delay, but now my experiences were almost synchronized with the act of reading.

It reached its peak a couple of days later when I was standing in the shower letting the water rush over me. It was one of those zen moments as I daydreamed under my personal waterfall. I don't know how long I stood there. The bathroom radio blared in the background, and I could hear bits of song over the roar of the showerhead. I remember opening my eyes under the stream of water and reaching for my shampoo bottle, a green, plastic job with curves like my girlfriend. Maybe my hands were soapy, but the container slipped from my fingers, and I nearly caught it twice before it crashed down on my big toe. I'd barely had time to cuss when I heard the singer on the radio crooning the words "I'm droppppping you...."

I'll call the singer C and the song W, but only because I could never track down the real names. I called up the radio station to find out, but it's one of those places that's operated by computer now.

For several days I tried to avoid reading anything. But that's not as easy as you might think. Go ahead and give it a try, and you'll see what I mean. Attempt to shop for groceries without reading the labels on the packages or the signs for the aisles. Or drive down the highway without looking at billboards. I can't even do my laundry without checking the tags on my shirts (cotton or permanent press? Machine or hang-dry?). And of course I always have to read stuff at work. But I tried to keep it to a minimum.

I was also trying to figure out the system. I'm a programmer. It's my job to know about algorithms. There had to be an ordering of events—a sequence of steps leading to certain effects. I could practically smell the pattern, although I couldn't quite nail it. All this had happened within a span of ten days. That's when I first read A's book Z, which had marked the beginning. Because I was avoiding print so thoroughly, my incidents were not frequent, but when they did occur, the connection between the reading and the experiencing was virtually instantaneous. I was perfectly in sync.

And then this: I was sitting in my apartment watching television when I noticed something odd sticking out behind the bookshelf—a kind of pale bulge, like a giant mushroom, a bizarre puffball growing from the crevice between the wall and the cabinetry. Given everything that had been happening, part of me felt I should ignore it, just turn away and pretend it wasn't there. The last thing I needed was to find some alien fungus growing in my living room. But what the hell. I got up to check it out, and when I pulled, out it popped—nothing more than a stuffed animal, the fluffy white whale my young nephew had with him when my brother's family came by a couple of weeks ago. As I stood up, I forgot myself, and my eyes fell upon the row of books on the middle shelf, where I happened to notice a gold title printed on black: *Moby-Dick*.

But I had found the whale *before* seeing the book. That is, the event had preceded the print. Wasn't that the opposite of how things had started?

This observation was confirmed over the next days: I'd see or do something, only to read about it shortly thereafter. For instance, in a fit of ferocity, my cat, Siegfried, scratched me. It was out of the blue, completely out of character. And then the morning paper arrived with the story of a tiger mauling a trainer during a Las Vegas act. Later I was driving around, running errands, when my rear brakes gave out; that afternoon I came across an article about compulsive behaviors—behaviors people can't *stop*. I read it three times. The whole thing was still eerie, yes, but the printed words no longer had any predictive value—they seemed only to repeat what had already happened. Then the confirmations started coming later and later, removed from the experiences they repeated in some slightly altered way. They became so remote—hours, and then days after the fact—that I lost track. I couldn't tell which things were being repeated, and which weren't. The density of experience made it too hard to keep up. Soon I was back to where I was.

I even went back to reading books. I finished reading *Z*. It was pretty good.

What had happened during that time? I still don't know. It seemed chaotic, although I sensed an order to it all. At the beginning it was the words that had come first, followed by the events. But then they crept closer and closer together, lining up almost, so what I read was like a caption for what happened. For the space of a couple of weeks I had found myself at the point of overlap, of synchronization. It has to happen sometimes, like a solar eclipse or the transit of Venus.

And then the whole thing had started to fade, just as it began. The world of deeds, traveling at a different speed, had slowly caught up with the world of words, and lapped it, moving further and further ahead, until it seemed they had never been aligned at all.

And now, while I wait for it to return, like Halley's comet,

I wonder idly about the scale of its cycles. Will I live to see it again? I find I'm nostalgic for those days when I could read the immediate future.

DONNY
DONNY

WE MET THE DAY the ambulance carried my mother away.

Summer was imminent and a game of freeze tag had just begun. Kids swarmed the yards, dodging outstretched hands, finding themselves petrified until friendly touches set them free. Brand new to the neighborhood, an awkward ten-year-old, I didn't even know the names of those who hunted me—I was simply grateful for the chance to be chased. Mammoth, our orange tabby, watched from the bushes, terror in her green eyes.

The first whine of the siren came while I balanced on one leg in the front yard, tagged in mid-stride. The sound swelled with every turn, and as the wail grew, kids gathered in the front yards. At last I let my foot drop, and my heart began to pound as the long nose of an ambulance slipped around the corner of our block. An emergency, right here, so close to home? Our move to such a privileged neighborhood struck me now as providential. The last stragglers joined our group and we stood in awe as the great vehicle approached and slowed, the blare of the siren winding down. It rolled to a stop just feet away, a spectacle designed just for us.

It's hard to pinpoint the instant when wonder dissolved into dread. Car doors slammed and two white-clad attendants rushed past, ignoring us as they headed up the steps to a house—the one I was just learning to call *mine*—the screen door creaking open and smacking shut behind them. Voices and shuffling sounded from within, along with heavy steps. Soon the door complained again, pressed to the side by one of the broad-shouldered men in hospital whites, backing out. Next came the horizontal form of my mother, laid out on a stretcher. As they carried her down to the sidewalk, she rolled her head in my direction, drawing her lips into a smile, her hair still perfectly in place, a small blond curl by her ear. She lifted the fingers of her left hand and hinted at a wave. My stomach ached, and the back of my neck shivered. I tried to swallow, but my throat wouldn't cooperate.

Then she was inside, and the doors slammed closed. The engine revved. Now the ambulance looked longer, had turned vast and solemn. The siren started its slow whine, and the vehicle pulled away. I surveyed our ragged group: all eyes were on me, all the mouths open in wonder. In the background, one of the neighborhood mothers was hustling across the yards in our direction, on a mission of consolation and control.

Only one among us seemed untouched by the drama. Sweeping his black hair to the side, Donny Wellek spoke his first words to me: "You see?" he said with a nod. "That's what happens when he sticks his thing in hers."

And he was right: I'd been slow to understand. No one had explained how it was supposed to work. Evidently the ambulance was standard procedure in 1968. The strange mom from two houses down supplied me with lunch and updates, the former heated from a can, the latter phoned in from the hospital.

All this to say that my mother's disappearance into the maw of the ambulance didn't lead to the dramatic future that had flowered briefly in my imagination. For an instant I'd pictured myself half-orphaned, pitied, suddenly singular and interesting. But Donny's comment had snapped me to, and I understood the course of events. When three days later the wrinkled, yellow creature thereafter known as my brother arrived home, I realized that I had indeed lost my mother—although not in the way I'd first imagined.

Michael's arrival was all the more precious for having come so late, ten years after my own appearance. Accordingly, I found myself not just dislodged from the center of the Ripple family universe, but relegated to the status of distant planetoid. Often I'd have to tuck myself in while my parents tended to the baby's bouts of colic. Or I'd eat breakfast alone, my mother too exhausted to crawl out of bed. My parents orbited around this new son, and since I still hadn't made friends in our neighborhood, Mammoth was the one I felt closest to. A fan of interesting smells, the cat got drunk on the fermented odors of my room, sleeping it off while sprawled across the harvest of dirty clothes. Sometimes I draped her over my shoulder like an enormous orange scarf. Whenever loneliness overwhelmed me, Mammoth made an excellent pillow into which to spill my tears.

Donny lived just two houses down. It was in part this proximity that brought us together, but also the fact that he was more accessible than other kids, less locked into the jigsaw puzzle of relationships. His availability should probably have sounded an alarm, but I was in need of companionship. Although a year older and nearly a foot taller, Donny was in my grade at school. His skin was oily, and strange, grown-up smells seeped from his body.

Through the first days of June we spent swaths of time playing Monopoly together, and many evenings we sat at one of the houses enjoying scenes from the far west. Lorne Greene and Michael Landon shot their way out of dilemmas we would find ourselves re-enacting in late afternoons, often armed with little more than fingers for six-shooters. Clayton Moore set high standards for honor as the Lone Ranger, occasionally outdone by the tragically misunderstood Chuck Connors in *Branded*.

Donny had a sharp eye for victims on these shows. "That one's going to get it," he'd say, pointing at some newcomer to the Ponderosa Ranch. The life expectancy of guest stars was short.

When we reproduced these tragic scenes outdoors, Donny always played the part of the bandit or the Indian—or whatever the TV had served up as the villain du jour.

Our programming of adventure was interrupted in early June when a man with a double name plugged three bullets into a presidential candidate in a hotel kitchen in California. I hadn't quite understood the function of a president, and I'd only seen Robert Kennedy a few times on TV. Scores of people had died from shootings in our living room before, but to my knowledge this was the only episode that had sent tears streaming down my mother's cheeks. She sat on the sofa, staring at the still pictures on the screen, clutching baby Michael to her breast, my father's arm around her shoulders. "Not again," she kept saying while rocking forward and back.

The assassination became grist for Donny's mill. Out in the yard, in a variety of situations, I obediently crumpled under my friend's sniper shots. He wanted me to call him Sirhan Sirhan, but I worried what Mom would say if she knew what we were playing at, so he settled for Donny Donny—a secret name, just between us. He liked having a sidekick.

Even more gripping than television was Donny's family, which appeared to be governed by wholly different laws than my own. Membership in our family included rules and chores, with my mother playing the role of sheriff. But the Welleks had given in to the forces of entropy. It wouldn't have surprised me if gravity itself ceased operation in the Wellek household. Donny's mother had brought no fewer than five Welleks into this world (which perhaps explained Donny's expertise in matters of reproduction) and the effort had apparently prompted her early retirement from the duties of motherhood. While my mom dusted, mopped, shopped and cooked, Mrs. Wellek drifted casually, like a hot air balloon. I did occasionally encounter her in their kitchen, but she was usually passing through to refill a gin and tonic before returning to her magazines or the telephone. Her children did not so much eat as graze, scrounging through the cupboards like modern hunter-gatherers, collecting handfuls of Cocoa Puffs or grasping at stray Pop-Tarts.

The kitchen was where I first encountered Donny's older sister, Sylvia, who one day slipped through wearing nothing but a towel, the bottom edge perfectly aligned with the rising curve of her buttocks.

"Get a load of that," Donny whispered to me as he indicated Sylvia's rump. Although I didn't think he should be as interested as I, I was grateful for the permission to stare.

Donny was my window to this other world—and, as I would soon learn, to galaxies beyond. In my own family sex belonged to the realm of the unspeakable, a part of an adult world that was well wrapped but not quite hermetically sealed. It had something to do with the gallantry of Zorro, when the women saved by the masked hero awoke from their swoons; one caught whispers of it in Rob and Laura's relationship on the Dick Van Dyke show; on occasion it even manifested itself in our own home, when Mom and Dad engaged in a rare and unhygienic smooch. Recently my mother mentioned that Mammoth was *in heat*, a strange expression that I couldn't decipher, and that was pre-empted two weeks later by her announcement that the cat was now pregnant. Mom volunteered vague answers to my pressing questions about this feline event.

The Wellek household offered a more thorough education, and I invited myself over with regularity, despite my ambivalence about a kid who'd call himself Donny Donny. But there was always the chance of glimpsing Sylvia in her towel. And Mr. Wellek was not above pinching and patting certain contours of his wife—who often positioned herself so as to encourage such molestations.

Donny enjoyed a kind of terrifying freedom. When he picked his nose he wiped the boogers on the wall of his room, just behind his bed—a stunt that would have cost me a limb back home. Then there was the time he showed me what a turd looked like as it emerged from the sphincter—a little number he referred to as "laying an egg." It was a fascinating sight, to be sure, but not a form of knowledge I could ever imagine passing on to others. Once, when Mammoth slinked past us in my backyard, her belly starting to round, Donny suggested that we cut her open to look at the babies. He followed it with a smile, but I wasn't sure he was joking.

He understood the scales of grown-up sentiment, and he played the notes with a mixture of ease and confidence. When there was trouble in the group, Donny was always in the area, but never pinned with the crime. One of the coarsest people I ever met, he had mastered the use of "sir" and "ma'am," powerful forms of address that gave him a patina of maturity and almost antebellum politeness of which few eleven-year-olds could boast.

These manners made him a convincing liar. When Jonas Trent's brand new transistor radio went missing at his birthday party, it was Donny who strode up to Jonas' mom. "Excuse me, ma'am," he said, his eyes bright, looking up from under a slightly furrowed brow, "but something has happened to Jonas's radio. Can you help us find it?" The fact that I later spotted the red plastic device in Donny's room did not surprise me. In fact, I admired the mask of deference and sincerity he had adopted so casually, not to mention the bold move by which he had placed himself above suspicion.

Donny and I were of different species, and I knew that his was the superior one, fitter for survival. His raw intelligence, unencumbered by academic achievement, remained a vast, untapped resource available for other, more illicit pursuits. When he introduced me to shoplifting, the victims of our spree consisted of the neighborhood shops lining Lake Avenue, only a few blocks from home. I lost my legal virginity at the Five and Dime on the corner, a slightly decrepit and over-stocked store run by Mr. Manning, a frail specimen of a bygone era, always decked out with a bow tie and red suspenders. Bird-like in his movements, he wore glasses of such abnormal thickness that they magnified his eyes twofold.

Donny gave me the essential instructions outside the store on a Saturday morning: Keep quiet and follow his lead. That was the sum of my lesson before he pushed through the jingling door, heading straight for the counter.

"Good morning, sir," Donny said, looking Mr. Manning in the eye.

"Good morning, boys," the old fellow croaked cordially.

I followed dumbly in Donny's wake. He scanned the comic book rack next to the register, picking out a *Batman* and perusing the opening pages. I kept waiting for the move, expecting him to slide the book up his shirt or to wad it into tiny balls in his cheeks, and my staring must have irritated him, because he pulled another comic off the rack and thrust it into my hands. I gaped at the pictures, turning the occasional page in an imitation of reading. My temples thundered and my fingers left small, sweaty smears on the pages.

At length Donny returned the comic book to the rack and moved on. Mr. Manning nodded as we headed to the back of the store, where we sidled past two women selecting cosmetics, past the toys and models, past the cleaning supplies, all the way back to stationery. There, in a smooth and discreet gesture, Donny slipped an elegant Parker pen out of its case and into his back pocket. All in all, the crime took mere seconds. Although I was on the brink of bolting, Donny dawdled. He stepped across the aisle to a stand of greeting cards. I'd seen enough movies to know that now was the time to run for it; in seconds the alarms would go off and sirens would sound in the distance. But Donny fingered the cards on display, stopping at some as if reflecting on their possible effect on the recipient. He selected a Get Well Soon card with a green envelope and headed up to the register. He actually slowed during his approach, as though eager to linger. As he leaned on the counter and began to chat with the smiling Mr. Manning, I could see the diagonal bulge of the pen in his back pocket.

"Find what you were looking for?" the old man asked.

"You have a wonderful card section," Donny replied.

Mr. Manning rang the purchase up. "Somebody you know not well?"

"My aunt," Donny said. "Aunt Lily. She broke... her collarbone."

Such a wonderful choice: not so banal as an arm or a leg, but more probable than a finger or a knee.

Coins were tendered and change received while Donny gave details of the imaginary accident of a make-believe person. The transaction completed, Mr. Manning looked over to me, his head canted slightly back so that his enormous eyes could bring me into focus through the bifocals.

"And anything for you, young man?" he asked.

As Mr. Manning's gaze drilled in, I sensed a flutter in my chest and my vision flickered. I feared I might black out entirely, leaving my small, felonious body collapsed on the linoleum of the Five and Dime. Off to the side I saw Donny dip his hand into a plastic bin of fingernail clippers, and in slow motion he slipped one into his front pocket. Always thinking, he was.

More than his success, I admired Donny's style. The principle of purchasing something at the same time you thieved made perfect sense, but the selection of a greeting card—that sign of selflessness and compassion for others—it put him absolutely above suspicion and elevated petty theft nearly to the realm of art.

Donny was unburdened by conscience, and his delight at playing with a newly palmed object was undimmed by the clouds of guilt that swirled about me. Still, I found the terror experienced in Manning's store strangely thrilling. Better than playing with fire—which was another pastime Donny introduced me to that summer—shoplifting was more like juggling with high explosives. In the unwritten criminal code of my home, burning down the house would have figured as little more than a misdemeanor in comparison to the capital offense of thievery.

Donny was gifted at stealing. And adventurous: we acquired some fine-looking tools from the hardware store, a large array of desk supplies from Manning's, and at one point he managed to smuggle a live neon tetra out of the pet store. And that was just from the neighborhood shops. Bit by bit Donny's room was starting to look like Ali Baba's cave, piled high with stolen treasures.

He gave me general pointers. Never linger in the back of the store: it gives rise to suspicion. And calculate your turns: if leaving the register requires you to show your left side, pocket your items on the right.

For my first solo job I settled on a prism from Manning's, a satisfyingly heavy pyramid of glass that divided the visible world into planes of light and color. Faithful to the teachings of the master, I made a purchase at the same time I stole, but I bungled my calculations: on my approach to the cash register, with Mr. Manning's unblinking fish-eyes peering down at me, our gazes met and locked. The surge of adrenaline left me light-headed. I willed myself to focus. In an attempt to allay suspicion I reached out to the nearest shelf, grabbing at random for a decoy purchase. At the register I found myself paying for an elegant pocketknife, priced at twice the cost of the prism. Red-faced under Mr. Manning's gaze, I spent precious moments counting out the coins while the lump of glass, hidden inside my sagging sock, threatened to tumble onto the floor.

The prism heist was not the only time I erred on the side of extravagance during my criminal adventures. In fact, this practice soon became more deliberate, for I discovered that larger purchases eased my conscience. Indeed, it occurred to me years later that Mr. Manning may have been wise to our operation but allowed it to prosper because it proved so good for business. Soon the bulk of my allowance was subsidizing my thievery. I could barely afford my life of crime.

Donny raised the stakes. In the back of Manning's, on the highest row of the magazine rack, there was a series of publications tucked behind a blue metal panel, above which only titles showed: *Penthouse, Vue, Gaze, Playboy....* At the time, the only magazine I knew intimately was *Boys' Life*, and to me the pinnacle of journalistic production was reached in the "Grin and Bear It" humor section found at the back of each issue.

The copy of *Gaze* that Donny smuggled out in his trouser leg was thus to shape the future course of my reading habits. The creatures I discovered in it shared only the slightest resemblance to women I had met in real life, but that shred of similarity was enough to pique my curiosity. I found myself studying candidates for comeliness in the world around me—and chief among these was Donny's sister. It was a stretch, but if anyone might grow into a model for *Gaze*, it was Sylvia Wellek.

I scrutinized girls with new interest, scoping out the Liddel twins from next door, and studying the brunette high-schooler who passed our house every afternoon. Even Mammoth's body, swelling with the promise of new lives, was subject to my investigations, made easier by the nakedness of animals. Clothing, I determined, was an obstacle. It played the same role as the blue metal panel on Mr. Manning's magazine rack, and I found myself yearning for the penetrating gaze reserved for superheroes.

Donny pointed me to a solution: the wrapper from a piece of Bazooka Joe bubblegum invited me to send in for "X-ray Specs," advertising that I'd be able to see people's bones beneath their clothing. It wasn't actually the skeletal structure that interested me, but the patter was vague about what was visible and what wasn't: "Look at your friend," the text read, "Is that really his body you 'see' under his clothes?" The ad gave us the benefit of the doubt, assuming we'd only use the specs for the knee-slapping camaraderie of male bonding. However, in the background of the gum wrapper they'd sketched a buxom female figure, her wink suggesting the manifold uses of this very practical joke. A dollar thirty-five and three weeks later, I received my eyewear, which I'd had them ship to Donny's address. But whom to select for my inaugural leer? My mother was always handy, but that idea barely had time to flicker in my consciousness before I banished it to oblivion. The obvious model would be Sylvia Wellek, and she obligingly posed before us as Donny and I passed the specs back and forth. Her ample forms yielded only a dark, fuzzy profile, which no amount of fiddling with the lenses or the lights seemed to remedy.

During this period I found myself devoured by remorse each time I headed home. I saw other kids out in the neighborhood, but they kept their distance. It was the same way they avoided my neighbor, as if he really were Donny Donny, a dangerous assassin. I would come into the house while Mom made chili or sloppy joes—my favorite dishes—but crime cut my appetite. At night, in my room, I buried my face in Mammoth's warm fur. The cat never judged me; she was happy with her imminent motherhood, purring as hard as she could to ease my misery.

I found myself purchasing ever larger items in the Five and Dime, and to swing this financially I was doing chores around the house for extra money. Most of my loot and many of the decoy purchases ended up in Donny's room—sometimes because I gave them to him for safe keeping, sometimes because he helped himself.

In August, I stopped stealing altogether: I couldn't afford it any longer.

I tried to disentangle myself from Donny, but he knew my weak spots. He used both the carrot and the stick: he made a gift to me of more dirty magazines, and once I accepted them he threatened to denounce me to my parents. Every day it was something new.

Then one evening he called me on the phone—a rare occurrence, since my back door was only a hundred feet from his.

"You got a sec?" he said, not even pretending it was a question. "Get over here right away. Come up quietly. I've got something for you."

The urgency in his voice made the invitation irresistible, and soon I was creeping up the stairs toward his room when his hand shot out of the darkness and pulled me in another direction.

"Keep real quiet," he hissed. "I think she's still in there."

Moments later he had led me down the hallway and into his parents' dark bedroom, his finger to his lips as we crept toward a door at the back. It was the second entrance to a main bathroom, and through the crack between the jamb and the poorly fitted door, there was an opening to which Donny and I applied our faces. Inside the steamy chamber, behind the mottled glass of the shower doors, we could see vague movement, flashes of skin. Although we could make out no discernible shape—not even the blurred masses perceptible with X-ray specs—there was an unmistakably naked body on the other side of the fogged glass, moving under a spray of water. Piled on the floor in front of the shower door was a large white towel, and I imagined how Sylvia had glided through the hallway to the bathroom, allowing the towel to slide off her body as she stepped under the streaming water. Flashes of color behind the glass gave rise to wild imaginings.

The mix of sensations visited upon me in that moment is difficult to describe: certainly a sweet and sudden hardening between my legs; just as surely a rush of excitement, and an irrepressible urge to stare. But there was the competing rise of panic and guilt. What was I doing here? What would my mother say? Then came a familiar itch at the back of my neck, and the room began to sway. I knew the wooziness would settle down if I closed my eyes, but Donny and I stood riveted to the spot. His hands were already busy below deck.

The shower water stopped, and we heard shuffling feet inside the stall. As Door Number One began to open for us, I went dizzy. First came the knee—less glorious than I'd imagined, to be sure, but a knee nonetheless. Next I caught a flash of muscled calf, a thigh of surprising darkness. And then something went terribly, terribly wrong.

That was it: after surprising Mr. Wellek in the shower, I knew it was time to reform. Like a bit actor showing up on yet another TV show, I would endow myself with a new personality. For starters, I stopped hanging out with Donny.

But it isn't always easy to do the right thing. In fact, it was not enough to set out on a new course: I had reparations to make. So I amassed some of the goods I had stolen and began a campaign of shop-putting. However, since I had already made use of many of these wares—having extracted them from their packaging and left them with traces of use—it was only fitting that I should repurchase them myself. The whole process turned frighteningly complex, far more perilous and considerably more expensive than the original heists. This was especially true at the Five and Dime, where I felt Mr. Manning's magnified eyes constantly on my back. Since I entered shops with concealed goods I had not yet purchased, I ran the risk of being accused of theft while in the midst of restitution. After depositing a stolen object back on its shelf, I would peel a sales sticker off a different article and apply it to the freshly returned one, which I could then carry up to the register and purchase.

My closest call came in the hardware store, where I mistakenly shop-put a cigarette lighter I had actually stolen from Manning's. The puzzled sales clerk was about to point out that it was not their merchandise, but then thought better of it and rang the lighter up anyway.

Once I crossed paths with Donny at Manning's. I was in the midst of returning a stapler, and I saw him slip a silver penlight into his pocket. He smiled at me and raised his eyebrows before turning to leave. I just shook my head: returning goods to Manning's was like trying to fill a leaky bucket.

The magazines were too precious to give away, and yet too dangerous to keep. I lived in fear that my mother, in some act of housecleaning zealotry, might discover my stash, and I would never manage to concoct a reasonable explanation for why so many photographs of breasts and buttocks had accumulated in the folder underneath the box of train track in the back of my closet. I needed to distance myself from this booty, so one night I snuck out into the yard and dug a shallow grave for these beautiful young women. I buried them in the garden, wrapped in plastic, using part of an old pea pole to mark the spot so I could find them when needed. I flinched at a noise in the bushes, and turned to see two luminous green eyes watching my every move. It was Mammoth. She'd lived up to her name, her belly huge and ripe, ready for birth. She turned and slunk away, moving slowly with her burden.

The world began to return to normal after I distanced myself from Donny. Although I missed our closeness, and felt a pinch of guilt for having abandoned him, I was glad to find myself playing more with other kids. The chains that had weighed on me for most of the summer began to lighten. By late August I was out again with the neighborhood group, relishing evening games of tag or capture the flag—although Donny rarely joined in. Sometimes I'd see him eyeing me from his yard as I ran with other kids. I would have preferred for him to swear at me, to insult me, so that I could hate him, but he just stood alone and watched, a solitary judge.

By late August the summer felt too long. I recall vividly the sensation of being frozen in tag—standing stock-still in the twilight, waiting for the touch of a friend to thaw me, to release me from my petrified state. For whole minutes I was arrested in time. Action whirled about while I practiced immobility. Sometimes the magic of this position—utter stillness in the midst of chaos, tinted with the anticipation of imminent release—sent a tingle down my spine, one that I wished to prolong, and which vanished as soon as a friendly finger freed me from my bondage.

This was the state I found myself in on the Friday evening before Memorial Day: poised in the darkness, listening to the crunch of footsteps on brittle grass and the sounds of television through open windows. The innocent hum of noises was rent by a screech of tires coming from the other side of the houses. I held my freeze as long as I dared while the others lit out. Car doors slammed. There came a buzz of voices, first the subdued chatter of children, followed by the more urgent tones of adults.

When I abandoned my pose and headed around to the front yard, a group stood by the curb. A long dark car I didn't recognize was stopped in the road. As I approached, faces turned and voices quieted. The group parted, opening a path to let me through.

On the asphalt Mammoth lay on her side, eyes half open, still. I stepped forward through the crowd as if in a game of freeze tag.

Everyone else had stopped; only I could go. If I touched them, they could move again. If I touched Mammoth, she would spring from her frozen state. But when I knelt down and felt her fur, my fingers worked no magic. Her pupils were but slits, even in the light of dusk, and the tip of her tongue showed between her teeth. I slipped my hands under her body and scooped her into my bare arms. She was perfectly intact. There was no blood. Nothing was broken. Her fur was soft and clean. But the unbearable limpness of the body told all. Her pregnant belly, full of promise, sagged, the tautness of life gone slack. When I stood and turned, I saw him in the crowd of kids, Donny, his lips pursed and his brow furrowed, a look poised between sympathy and satisfaction.

THE
BIRTHDAY
LIST

I COULD USE some new socks. You know the kind. And maybe a pair of gloves. I wouldn't mind a copy of that CD I told you about. And perhaps a novel or two, but only if they're worth reading.

That's about it.

Well, I also want to go out. Anywhere. For dinner, a movie, whatever. And not just for my birthday. Generally. I want to go to museums. I want to learn things. I want a change of scenery. I want to move.

And how about a new pen? A nice one, preferably blue, with a fine point. I'll need some stationery to go with it. Some Post-its, so I can leave you notes. I want a phone. One that works. Or a megaphone. Walkie-talkies. I want two empty tin cans tied together by a waxed string.

What I mean is that I want you to listen to me.

And for me to listen to you.

I want us to look at one another. I want us to stop walking through each other's shadow feeling nothing more than a chill.

I want a new job. I want friends again, the kind who stay up all night talking. I want to be younger. I want to turn off the news. I want not to worry about the future of the planet. I want politicians to stop being idiots.

I want to feel at home. I want you to love me the way you used to. And I want to return the favor.

I want our dead to be alive again. I'd like my whole life resuscitated. I want not to have wished for that. I want to forget. I want to remember. I want to live forever. I want to die, right now.

I want to know what happened. What I did. What I can do.

I want to know why it turned out this way. I need to know if it's too late.

I want you to know that I tried. I hope you appreciate how hard it has been. I want you to forgive me, and I want to be able to forgive you.

I wish all this could go without saying. If only you could read my thoughts—then at least one of us would understand.

All I really want is: *something*. I'm afraid I can't be more specific. Whatever you think will work. Nothing too expensive.

And if at all possible, I'd love for it to be a surprise.

ACKNOWLEDGEMENTS

Many people offered crucial support, advice, and encouragement at various stages of the writing of *This Jealous Earth*, especially: Anne Maple, Michael Kidd, Greg Johnson, Matt Bell, Laura Goering, Jim Burgett, Dale Gregory Anderson, Mark Breitinger, Anne Ulmer, Sigi Leonhard, and Victoria Skurnick. At MG Press I'd like to recognize Robert James Russell and Jeff Pfaller for their many contributions, Bailey Shoemaker Richards for her sharp eye and pencil, and Sarah E Melville for cover art that still gives me goose bumps.

My thanks to you all.

Many of the stories in this book first appeared (often in slightly different form) in other venues: "The Birthday List," in *Every Writer Resource Short Stories* (Sept. 20, 2011), reprinted in *Eunoia Review* (January, 2012) and *The Carleton Voice* (Winter, 2012); "Donny," in *Ducts*, Issue 24 (Winter 2010), reprinted in *Midwestern Gothic* (Fall, 2012); "General Relativity," published as an audiocast at Lit-Cast.com (November, 2007); "Sincerely Yours," in *Ducts*, Issue 20 (Winter 2008); "Foundering," in *Prime Number* (Issue 13.2, October, 2011); "Future Perfect," in *Short Fiction Collective* (November 7, 2011); "The Visit," in slightly different form in *Spilling Ink*, Issue 7 (December, 2011); "The Phrasebook," in *Red Ochre Press* (December, 2011); "Riddles," in *Anomalous* (December, 2011); "Inheritance," in *Midwestern Gothic* (Winter, 2012); "The Spirit of the Dog" (*The MacGuffin*, Spring/Summer 2012); "Thrift" in *Chamber Four* (Fall, 2012).

Scott Dominic Carpenter was born in Minneapolis but grew up on the move. After proving himself ill-suited to mining, factory work, and other forms of hard labor, he took refuge in libraries and classrooms, many of them in Madison, Wisconsin. He teaches French literature and critical theory at Carleton College (MN), but in addition to his scholarly work, he commits fiction, examples of which have appeared in venues like *Chamber Four, Ducts, Midwestern Gothic, The MacGuffin, Prime Number* and *Spilling Ink,* as well as in the anthology *Best Indie Lit New England.* A Pushcart Prize nominee and a semi-finalist for the MVP Competition from New Rivers Press, he will soon release a debut novel (*Theory of Remainders*, Winter Goose Publishing). His website is located at: http://www.sdcarpenter.com.

16615782R00119

Made in the USA
Charleston, SC
02 January 2013